What is a Strebor Quickiez? Years ago, I decided that I wanted to create a series of short, erotic books that would be designed to be read in the span of one day. Thus, the Strebor Quickiez collection was born. Whether a reader takes in the excitement on the way to and from work on public transportation, or during their lunch break and before bedtime, they can get a "quick fix" in the form of a stimulating read.

Designed to be published in collections of three to six titles per season, Strebor Quickiez will be enticing to those who steer away from larger novels and those who do not have the time to commit to spend a longer span of time to take in a good read. The first set includes *The Raw Essentials of Human Sexuality*, *One Taste* and *Head Bangers: An APF Sexcapade*; the follow-up to my wilder successful novel *The Sisters of APF: The Indoctrination of Soror Ride Dick*. Rounding out the collection is a trilogy featuring three women who receive separate invitations to make their respective sexual fantasies come true: *Obsessed*, *Auctioned* and *Disciplined*.

It is my hope and desire that booksellers embrace Strebor Quickiez and promote them to their consumer base. I am convinced that these books can do a heavy volume in sales and, as always, I appreciate the support shown to all of my efforts throughout the eight years.

Blessings,

Zane

ALSO BY ZANE

The Sex Chronicles: Shattering the Myth
Addicted
Shame On It All
The Heat Seekers
Nervous
Skyscraper
Gettin' Buck Wild: Sex Chronicles II
The Sisters of APF
Afterburn
Dear G-Spot
Blackgentlemen.com
Another Time, Another Place
Zane's Sex Chronicles
Love is Never Painless

EDITED BY ZANE

Breaking the Cycle
Chocolate Flava
Succulent: The Eroticanoir.com Anthology
Caramel Flava
Honey Flava
Purple Panties
Missionary No More

A NOVEL

HEAD BANGERS
An APF Sexcapade

NEW YORK TIMES BESTSELLING AUTHOR

SBI

STREBOR BOOKS

NEW YORK LONDON TORONTO SYDNEY

SBI

Strebor Books
P.O. Box 6505
Largo, MD 20792
http://www.streborbooks.com

ISBN-13 978-1-59309-239-9
ISBN-10   1-59309-239-3
LCCN 2008938021

First Strebor Books trade paperback edition May 2009

Cover design: www.mariondesigns.com
Cover photograph: © Keith Saunders/Marion Designs

10   9   8   7   6   5   4   3

Manufactured in the United States of America

For information regarding special discounts for bulk purchases, please contact Simon & Schuster Special Sales at 1-866-506-1949 or business@simonandschuster.com

The Simon & Schuster Speakers Bureau can bring authors to your live event. For more information or to book an event, contact the Simon & Schuster Speakers Bureau at 1-866-248-3049 or visit our website at www.simonspeakers.com.

DEDICATION
For Jewell

Women are the new men.

For far too long, we have allowed the male species
to assume that they rule the world.

That they are somehow more essential to us breathing
oxygen than vice versa.

But the fact of the matter is that pussy, not dick,
controls everything under the sun.

Men will rob, steal, cheat, murder and even
go to war over pussy.

The idiots still do not think we realize it.

The days of sisters taking any kind of
bitchassness from men are over.

We are independent, successful, brilliant,
and a thousand times more essential than them.

Fuck a man shortage.

Fuck bowing down and being submissive.

We will do what we want, when we want,
and no one will tell us any different.

The sexual revolution is here to stay.

WOMEN ARE THE NEW MEN!

ALPHA PHI FUCKEM-
THE CONVENTION

"Ooops, I'm sorry, Miss!" We both reached for the lettuce tongs on the supermarket salad-bar island at the same time. "Ladies first!"

"No, you go right ahead. I insist." I was checking his ass out, and he was too damn fine.

He smiled at me, and I wanted to take a ride on his black pony. "You sure?"

"Yes, you were here first."

He started getting his iceberg lettuce, and I kept getting my peep on. He was about six-one, 200 pounds of solid muscle with chocolaty smooth skin and was sporting the roundest, firmest butt I had ever seen.

"Can I ask you a question?" He looked at me, probably thinking I was going to ask him the time of day or something normal. He couldn't have been further off base. The convention had snuck the hell up on me, and time was of the essence for me to find a playmate for the upcoming weekend. "Are you married?"

He blushed. "No, I'm not. You?"

"No." We stood there smiling at each other, but there was no salad-fixing going on. "Engaged? Shacking up?"

"No. None of the above."

Excerpted from *The Sex Chronicles: Shattering the Myth* (Pocket Books, 2002)

It was time to go for it. Patricia already had her partner for the weekend, as did all the other sorors in the D.C. chapter. I had been so busy pulling long hours in the courtroom that I hadn't had a chance to go dick hunting. "I see. I was just wondering what you're doing this weekend."

He started blushing even harder. I got the impression he was used to being the hunter and not the hunted. "I'm supposed to go over to one of my boys' houses to watch the fight on pay-per-view, but that's about it."

"You can never tell with those fights. Sometimes they only last a couple of minutes."

We were flirting, no damn doubt about it, but I didn't want a man for a relationship. I had one of those already. However, taking him to the convention was out of the damn question. He knew my name and everything about me, and that's against the rules. The sacred vows of Alpha Phi Fuckem must never be broken. *Never!*

"You're so right about that! The last fight I saw only lasted a few seconds. If you blinked, you missed it."

"Hmmm, I see. Well, the fight might only last a few seconds, but I can ride your dick all night long."

He almost dropped the salad container he was holding onto the floor but caught it as it ricocheted off the edge of the counter. He cleared his throat and gave me the most perplexed look. "Is that right?"

"Damn skippy." I didn't have time for all the bullshit. Either he was going to be the one or he wasn't, so I got straight to the point. "Listen up, boo. It's like this."

He was grinning like a wino that just found a bottle of un-opened Mad Dog 20/20 in a garbage can. "Yes?"

"My sorors and I are having our national convention in Atlantic

City this weekend, and I was wondering if you're up for a fuckfest?"

"Excuse me?" He started choking. On what, I have no idea. "Did you say fuckfest?"

"Uh-huh. Fuckfest!"

He cleared his throat, wondering how he ended up having such a blessed day. "What sorority are you in? AKA? Delta? Sig—"

"Nope, none of that." I was hoping he wouldn't pass the hell out when I told him the truth. The brother's nerves seemed a bit on edge, but I like them timid sometimes. "The name of my sorority is Alpha Phi Fuckem."

That did his ass in. "Oh, come off it. This is a joke, right?"

"No, not at all." He started looking around as if he thought I was working for *Candid Camera* and trying to play a trick on his ass. "I'm for real. I want you to accompany me to Atlantic City this weekend and knock some boots."

"DAMN!" He had that look they all have—the one they get when they realize that we're not bullshitting and just want some dick carte blanche without the attachments.

"Look, are you down or what?"

"Hold up, baby. You never even told me your name. I'm—"

I put my finger to his lips. "You're my cumdaddy, and you can just call me Soror Ride Dick."

Well, by the time the last crouton hit the top of my blue cheese dressing, it was a done deal. I told my cumdaddy to meet me along with the rest of the crew behind Iverson Mall the next evening at 6 P.M. sharp to get on the bus for Atlantic City. The sorors and I opted not to fly or drive different cars and decided to charter a bus instead. We wanted to get a bit freaky on the way up there, and boy, did we!

The D.C. chapter now has thirty members instead of just twenty-four. It was a real tight squeeze on the bus with all the sorors and their playmates on board, but the more, the merrier. Some sorors sat on laps, with or without the man's dick whipped out and inserted, and Soror Lick 'Em Low, a new inductee who has a thing for sucking on balls, got her freak on in the tiny lavatory of the bus.

The bus driver, Ralph, was the happiest man alive on the way up and almost wrecked, between trying to see what we were doing and glancing at the porno tapes we were playing on the tiny television screens throughout the bus. Soror Voyeur was responsible for providing the videos. She has quite the collection, so it was mad interesting.

We all got fucked up on the way up, and I literally got fucked too. My cumdaddy shed all his inhibitions, flipped my ass over one of the plush seats, and banged me slowly from behind while I sipped on a Bartles & Jaymes. Patricia's playmate was a male stripper she picked up at some thug club. I could tell she was going to have problems with his ass all weekend. He was smoking so much weed that he had trouble keeping a hard-on while she was sucking his dick on the bus.

When we got to Atlantic City about 10 P.M., most of the other chapters had already arrived and settled in at the casino hotel. NYC, L.A., and Atlanta were strongly representing. Those three chapters seem to grow by leaps and bounds every year and have at least fifty members each. Detroit is up to about fifteen members now, and Chicago has about twenty. The Miami sorors had yet to arrive, but their plane was due in before midnight. They are about a dozen members strong.

The biggest surprise came out of left-fucking-field when we met the members of our new chapters from Nashville, Tennessee, and Atlantic City. The two chapters worked together to plan and host this year's convention, and to say the new sorors are a bit out there is a serious understatement. They're fucking wild, and you know that's deep if I am saying it.

They had all the room keys already, so none of the men could get our real names from the registration desk. In fact, we were all registered under aliases anyway, so it wouldn't have mattered much. I still had to admire the lengths of discretion the new sorors went to. What was even more appreciated were the toys they strategically placed in all the hotel rooms. Instead of breath mints on the pillows, there were dildos, edible panties, and a pair of shiny new handcuffs on each bed to enhance the weekend's activities.

In the bathrooms, along with the shampoo, soap, and toothpaste provided by the hotel, were baskets full of scented body oils, liquid latex, butt plugs, and anal beads. They also had a bottle of champagne chillin' in every soror's room. It was the bomb, and I knew the weekend would be the shit.

The main activity of the night didn't start until 1 A.M., so cumdaddy and I made good use of time by taking a hot shower and doing the flying 69 in the warm stream of water. He turned me upside down and ate out my pussy while I sucked his dick. The water hitting up against my clit and his tongue action made me cum at least three times before we hit the bed and destroyed all the effort the hotel maid had put into making it up neatly. For about an hour, I did what I do all too well and rode the hell out his dick.

We were exhausted but woke up a little when we took another quick shower to get dressed for casino night. At 1 A.M., the happenings began in a private casino of the hotel. As soon as everyone hit the door, all the clothes had to come off. We enjoyed a night of playing blackjack, poker, roulette, and craps in the nude. By prearrangement with the hotel, all the cocktail waitresses and dealers were nude too—just a bigass room full of butt-naked people, and it was all good.

Instead of cashing in chips for money, you had to cash in your chips for sexual favors from the person of your choice. That's when the shit got real interesting, 'cause the sorority ended up having the biggest orgy in its history that night. People were fucking anywhere they could find a spot. I fucked three men at the same time on top of the green velvet cloth on a craps table while my cumdaddy fed his dick to two of the new sorors from the Nashville chapter. They were all on him, and I thought they were about to come to blows over it, because they were both being so damn greedy with the dick. Can't say I blame them, though, 'cause the brotha did have some good-ass dick.

I enjoyed myself immensely. A dick in the hand, one in the mouth, and one in my pussy beats two in the bush any damn day. By the time 6 A.M. rolled around and the sunlight began to stream in through the skylights of the private casino, we were all ass-out, dicks and tits and ass everywhere.

We were served brunch in our respective hotel rooms about noon and then set out at 3 P.M. to head to a private spa. There, the hosting sorors had us all pampered with full-body massages, and different people enjoyed sexing each other down in various hot tubs, saunas, and massage rooms.

Cumdaddy and I had a great time making love on a massage table with the ceiling fan going full speed overhead. Both of our bodies were still silky smooth and tingling from the body masks we were given. I'm sure you can probably guess who was on top. They don't call me Soror Ride Dick for nothing.

At 8 P.M. Saturday evening, we got down to business, and it

was the only time any of us were fully clothed the whole weekend. We had our banquet in a ballroom at the hotel, all dressed in formal wear. The men all had on tuxedos, and the sorors were all decked out in the latest fashions. I wore a skintight black sleeveless gown with a split going all the way up the back and no panties. What can I say? I have this thing about walking around coochie-free, and so I did. In fact, my cumdaddy and I played a little game to see how tight my pussy muscles really were and how much control I have over them. He put a pair of Ben Wa balls in my pussy before we left the room and bet me I couldn't walk around all night with no panties on and keep them from falling out.

The keynote speaker was from the old school of sorors. We call her Soror Love Lace because she wears something made of lace 90 percent of the time. She's actually an investment banker, and she went over the investment strategies and agenda for the national chapter's combined assets. The evening was informative and enlightening as we dined on lobsters, scalloped potatoes, and string beans almondine.

After the banquet was over, most of the sorors went clubbing at another hotel a little way down the boardwalk. Since I won the bet and kept the balls in place all night, I collected on it and made cumdaddy suck on my pussy under the moonlight on the beach for a good hour before we joined the others.

We turned that mother-fucking club out too. They were expecting us to be stuck-up and snobbish because of the way we were dressed. Instead, we ended up scaring half of the sexually repressed customers away and putting on one hell of a show for the ones who stuck it out. The Nashville sorors got up on the stage and started freaking all over one another and ripping each other's expensive gowns off while the rest of us cheered them on.

After they were all in their birthday suits, they had a dance competition and a sexy body contest. The winner was awarded a twelve-inch dildo in a black velvet box, and the runner-up received a gold-plated vibrator with an anal sleeve. The sorors from Nashville are my type of peeps. I was digging it.

We finished the evening off by having a *Soul Train* line in the nude. There were mad dicks doing the Bankhead Bounce coming down the aisle, and I was admiring every one of them. We had a beautiful dick contest, and I was proud when my cumdaddy took the honors and received a golden dick trophy. I bet he's still showing that shit off to his friends now.

We all went back to our rooms about 2 A.M. and did whatever was clever. I spent the last few hours with my cumdaddy, getting to know him better in three ways: mentally, physically, and orally. It's a damn shame we can never keep any of the bomb-ass dick we run across. Sometimes I wish the rules were different, but a vow is a vow is a vow, and I will never break it.

The majority of us were so fucked out that we slept most of the way home on the bus. When we got back to Iverson Mall, I almost got emotional when it was time to say goodbye. Patricia had to practically drag my ass to the car. I maintained my composure in the end, waved farewell to cumdaddy, and went home to my man. When he asked me how the antitrust law seminar in Richmond, Virginia, went that weekend, I simply replied, "Awesome!" It damn sure was. Soror Ride Dick, over and out!

SOROR RIDE 'EM HIGH
AND
SOROR LICK 'EM LOW

FAITH

"Ladies, you are looking too hot for words!" Raheem yelled at us as we started pulling all of our shit out of our Hummer H3.

Big vehicle or not, we had a lot of crap, mostly because Hope did not believe in leaving a single outfit in her closet back at home. The drive from Atlanta had been a scorcher. Gas was higher than caviar and there was no way we were going to run the air conditioner. Thus, the ten-hour drive had found us bickering with each other and pondering whether to open cans of whup ass on some of the other drivers on the road. I reminded Hope about this Lifetime movie where these two Canadian women got involved in a road rage incident after one made the other miss an exit in rush-hour traffic. One of them ended up shot to death, leaving behind a disabled son, and the other ended up missing a leg and possibly going to prison, leaving her yet unborn child and other kids to be raised by their father. After we remembered that nonsense, we calmed down but we were still going at each other.

"Thanks, Raheem," Hope said seductively, poking out her ta-tas in her red tank top. "You're looking good yourself."

I rolled my eyes as I attempted to yank Hope's big-ass duffel bag out the backseat. "He would look ten times better helping us with these damn bags," I stated sarcastically.

Raheem pretended like he did not even hear me. Lazy ass!

Licking his lips at Hope, who had stopped helping me also, he asked, "So which one are you? Aren't you Faith?"

Hope sucked her lips and blew out a puff of air. "Damn, you can't tell us apart yet? I'm the fly-ass one," she responded.

"Yeah, she has flies all up in her ass," I said. I slapped Hope on the back of her head.

"Ouch, Faith!"

"We can't leave this truck double-parked here the entire day. Look at all these peeps trying to move into the dorm. You can flirt with Mr. Chivalry later. He can take you out and watch you open up the doors and pull out chairs for him."

"Cute, Faith," Raheem said. "Now I can tell which is which. You're always so bitter."

"I'm not bitter. I simply fail to see the point of wasting conversation on little boys."

"I'm nobody's boy!"

"Well, you sure aren't anybody's man. Last time I checked, a real man would not stand there and watch two women drag a bunch of luggage into a building."

Now you would think that my pointing that out to old boy would have persuaded him to help. Instead, he hauled ass.

"I've gotta jet." Raheem started backing away from us. "I have a football team meeting in a few."

I stood there and watched Hope staring him down as he walked away, like he was a piece of black licorice.

"He is too fine," she said.

"And he's a piece of shit," I added. "Why do you insist on fooling around with subhumans? He probably has a tiny wing-wing, too."

Hope glared at me. "First of all, I have never fucked Raheem."

"But you're thinking about it. You can't fool me; I'm your

damn twin and I know how you think and how you look when you're ready to give up some pussy out both sides of your drawers."

"Humph, well, that's my business. And, besides, I heard he has an anaconda in his shorts."

"I bet that rumor came straight from his lips."

"Stop hating."

"I'll stop hating if you start helping me with this stuff. Three-fourths of it is yours anyway. We could have shared some clothes, if you wanted to mix things up. You're such a label whore. None of these designers are giving you royalties for pimping their shit. This doesn't make any sense. It's not like we left the United States. We only left Atlanta and we're going home for Thanksgiving."

"Blah, blah, blah," Hope said, pushing my buttons. She knew I hated it when people started all that "blah, blah, blah" shit.

Some other males started walking in our direction. Hope began playing with her hair and poking her tits out again. That did it for me. I slammed the cargo door of the Hummer shut and stomped off.

"Where the hell do you think you're going?" she called after me.

"I'll be in the room."

"What about all this stuff?"

"Get your approaching dick action to bring it up. I'm going to take a nap."

"Faith, that's fucked up."

I laughed but refused to turn around and look at her. I gave her the finger. "Life is fucked up."

I decided to let Hope be the prey for the land sharks heading her way. She was totally in her element.

HOPE

Faith was amusing. She always tried to portray some holier-than-thou, good girl role in front of the other students at school. Yet, she was the one who had insisted that we join Alpha Phi Fuckem our sophomore year. Now that we were seniors, she was on an emotional roller coaster. I think she was concerned about where we would both end up after college. Our entire lives, since the womb, we had been inseparable, but things were likely to change. We had not majored in the same thing so there was zero chance of us working for the same corporation upon graduation. I majored in journalism, because I had always been nosey as all get out, and Faith's major was chemical engineering. She was eyeing a great entry-level position at DuPont in Belle, West Virginia, but I could not envision it. The thought of my twin in West Virginia was mind-boggling. No way were those hillbillies prepared for her ass.

While we were younger, maybe as long ago as when we were seven or eight years old, I discovered that Faith had two sides to her. She would act a certain way to please our parents, devout Christians who got married right out of high school and probably had never fucked anyone other than each other their entire lives. Faith would do everything right, kiss up to them, and do whatever they said… while they were watching. Behind their backs, she was hell on wheels. She would do her dirt, blame it on me, and then threaten me with physical violence if I refused to be "the bad seed."

By the time we were thirteen, Faith was ready to fuck little boys to death. She didn't though, but only because they couldn't get their dicks in her. When we got a little older, I was reading this article about women who have sexual issues and I believe that Faith had some sort of psychological block that prevented it. Ironically, I "technically" lost my virginity two months before she did. The crazy part is that I had no intention of even having sex. I can't claim that is was a "he slipped and fell in" moment because it took some effort for him to burst my cherry. What I mean is that the guy that I gave my most precious jewel to was not even on my radar a few hours before it happened.

It was Homecoming Weekend at our high school, B.E. Mays, and this boy named Jacob was visiting his cousin Thomas from Alabama. Since Atlanta is not that far from Alabama, I had heard all kinds of rumors about "Alabama Black Snake." In fact, Faith and I were so gullible back then that we both actually believed that there was something special, damn near extraterrestrial, about black men and their dicks that lived in Alabama. We were not alone either. When Jacob showed up at one of the house parties, girls were drooling all over themselves to get at his fine ass. I was still kind of shy so I was in the corner, hoping someone would ask me to dance. My favorite cut was on: "Hot in Herre" by Nelly. It was damn sure hot up in that bitch, too. Peeps were pushed up on each other from wall to wall.

Faith was smack dab in the middle of the floor, grinding on Marcus, one of the fools who had been trying to ram his dick in her for ages. I was moving my hips slightly from side to side and then I saw Jacob walking toward me. I almost creamed in my panties. He had this swagger about him and he had the legendary "black snake" between his Alabama legs.

"What's up, sweetness?" he asked in a country-bumpkin tone.

I almost cringed but smiled instead. His teeth were crooked. His case of "gaposis" was messing up his fineness a little and sounding like Elmer Fudd did not enhance him either. But he still looked good, standing there in some jean shorts, a red T-shirt that said "All my nuts are creamy" and some Air Force Ones. He had a close crop, he was dark-skinned and had these huge, intriguing, nearly black eyes.

"Just chillin'," I replied, looking from left to right, trying to avoid eye contact. I hated it when boys stared at me. Now that I am older, I find it sexy, but not back then. I always felt like they were trying to spot my imperfections. "Listening to the music."

"You wanna dance?"

Before I could respond, he was yanking me toward the middle of the floor, next to Marcus and Faith. He started grinding up against me and I was confused. I didn't feel anything. *Where was the damn snake?*

He glanced at Faith. "Dang, I thought I was seein' double at first."

That was a stupid-ass statement. He *was* seeing double. I decided to enlighten him. "We look exactly alike, so you are seeing double."

"Daggone it. You'se right."

Faith started grinning at me and poking me in the ribs. I knew what she was doing. I was always kind of frigid when it came to dancing, even if I loved the music. Faith had video whore written all over her. She was damn near a contortionist on the dance floor and the guys could not get enough of watching her put in work.

We danced for another good hour and I was getting heated, from Jacob rubbing all over my ass. When "U Got It Bad" by Usher was on, I thought he was trying to crack my back. That was when I finally felt something: the snake.

Faith announced that she was leaving with Marcus, and thus,

leaving me stuck. I am not going to lie. We had plenty of friends at the party that could have taken me home but I wanted to see what was up with Jacob. He told me that he had a car outside.

"Cool," I said, when he asked if he could give me a ride.

"So, you g to g?"

"Huh? G to g?"

"Good to go."

I laughed because I had never heard that shit before. Jacob had a strange way of expressing himself. I was about to find out exactly how much.

His car was cool. A typical *Dukes of Hazzard*, kitted out Dodge Charger with a bunch of after-market parts and a bright ass red paint job. He had chrome running gear, blue lights attached to the undercarriage, tinted wheels, deck stripes, twenty-inch wheels, and a gold chain framing his license plate that read: "G Style." The engine sounded like a jet plane.

"You better not ever try to commit a crime in this car," I joked as he closed the door and I settled into the passenger seat. "If they can't see you a mile away, they can damn sure hear you."

Jacob chuckled. "Please, I know how to C.M.A."

"C.M.A.?"

"Cover my ass."

Once we took off, he asked, "You wanna head straight home or you wanna sammich? We can go to macadoodledandys."

Finally, I knew what his country ass was talking about. "No, thanks. McDonald's messes with my stomach. I'm watching my weight."

"Sweetness, as fine as you are, someone would have to pull a MacGyver to damage you." He reached over and touched my leg. "You damn sure ain't a salad dodger."

"A salad dodger." He was about to answer but I quickly said,

"Never mind." It was becoming stressful to carry on a conversation.

Once we got to our street, Jacob asked me if he could park down at the dead end so we could rap for a minute.

"You sittin' over there, looking all sexified." He undid his seatbelt, then mine, and leaned over toward me. "Those lips. Damn, those lips look so sexy."

Next thing you know we were kissing. Well, I was trying to kiss but he was so sloppy and aggressive with it, that once we came up for air, I felt like there was a lick tide all over my face. Once I finished wiping my face off with my sleeve, I debated about getting out of the car and walking down the street. I saw Marcus' Camaro pulling into our driveway. Faith hopped out and dashed inside. She must have been mad. No kisses. No hugs. Just out the car and in the house. He must not have been able to get the dick in yet again.

"Your sis is home, huh?"

He was such a freaking genius!

"I head back to Bama tomorrow," Jacob said. "I wanna see you again."

I did not respond. I was still debating. Part of me had been yearning to get rid of my virginity. I wanted to get it over with because I realized the first time was not going to be the moon, the sun and the stars, even if I was in love.

"There will be pain," my friend, Kim, had informed me. Kim was the resident expert at our school. Every boy found her *lustworthy*, even though she was a "long back." She had no ass to be found but her humongous tits made up for it. We used to take bets on how many boys at Mays had been breastfed by Kim. That was her claim to fame. That and sucking dick. I was definitely not ready to suck a dick but, hell, I wanted to get the penetration thing over with.

"Let's fuck," I announced, as casually as if I had said, "Let's bake a batch of brownies."

"You for real?" Jacob asked.

I started pulling my top over my head. "Drive over to the next street. There's a park. I don't want to do it here. Our neighbors might see something and tell my folks."

I did not have to instruct him twice. We gave "gone in sixty seconds" a new meaning because his loud-ass ride was parked behind a tree in less than thirty.

He tried to kiss me again but I did not feel like becoming a drowning victim, so I turned my head away and started pecking on his neck as we helped each other get out of our clothes. I climbed over into the backseat. He slapped me on the ass and licked my right buttock and then followed behind me.

"I bet you're a pro," he said, not realizing that I had never had a dick intake experience in my life.

"Just shut the hell up." I pulled his head down to my breasts, hoping he would figure out what I wanted. He did and started sucking on my nipples. It felt like a waterfall was cascading down my sides; there was so much slobber.

I reached down to feel his dick and I do not know if it was a snake, but it was not a big-ass snake if it was. I also did not know what made Alabama dick special, being as I had never seen or touched a dick. I was ready to get it over with though.

"Stick it in," I said. "But you have to wear a condom."

He sighed, reached over the seat and retrieved a Headstrong condom from his shorts pocket. I watched him put it on.

He spread my legs, placed my calves on his shoulders and

tried to shove it up in me in one fell swoop. I practically screamed but bit my bottom lip and held it in.

"Damn, sweetness, you tight," Jacob said. "Let me loosen you up a bit."

Before I knew it, Jacob had his head buried between my legs and was trying to suck my ovaries clear out. I squirmed and held onto the front headrest with one hand and the top of the backseat with the other. I was moaning and flopping around like a fish in the backseat. From that very second, I realized that whatever man that I ended up with, he would have to love to eat pussy.

It was not clear to me, whether or not I had an orgasm, but the backseat was soaked. It could have been his spit, my pussy juice or a combination. Whatever it was, the shit felt good.

He ate me out for about ten minutes and then started trying to get his dick in again. I relaxed and cleared my head. I looked up at the stars through the rear window and told myself that I could do it. I could let this country bumpkin fill me up with his Alabama black snake and live to see another day. I took a deep breath, stopped clamping my ass cheeks shut, and he was all up in there. He went to stroking and I held back my screams, thinking, *Thank goodness his dick is no bigger than it is!* I would have had to fake a leg cramp if he was any larger.

Jacob started whispering some shit that I could never even make out while he was doing calisthenics with his dick inside of me. I could tell that he was not that experienced, especially since he had yet to figure out that I was a virgin.

It seemed like we were fucking for hours when, in essence, it was only about five minutes. He exploded inside the Headstrong and I was speechless. *Damn, the power of the pussy!* I had heard that men can be controlled by pussy; the pursuit of it or the urge for it. Seeing Jacob's face in the moonlight said it all. That shit was true. If I could master the art of fucking, men would do whatever the hell I wanted.

We got dressed and I made Jacob take me home, promising that I would call him the next day. That was not to happen but I needed to get rid of him. I did not want any ties, any delusions and there definitely were no feelings. Hell, I did not even know his ass. Just that he used weird slang to say normal shit, thinking it was cool when it was truly irritating. I could not imagine trying to carry on daily phone conversations with him. If he could simply come to town, commence to fucking and leave, that would have been one thing. The way he was talking, he wanted an assurance that I would be his girlfriend. He was more than likely spitting game but I was not going to risk it. I gave him a kiss on the cheek after he walked me to the door, avoiding any more sloppy tongue action, and that was that.

Faith was waiting up for me. After I told her that I had fucked, she said, "Shit, I knew that already!"

"What do you mean? You knew it."

"I felt it in my pussy."

"Get the fuck out of here!" I exclaimed, almost waking our parents. I was surprised that they had slept through Jacob's loud engine in the first place. I lowered my voice. "You didn't feel a damn thing."

"I'm serious," Faith said. "We're connected. Think about it. We have our periods the same exact days and…"

I interrupted her. "That has nothing to do with us being twins. It is a known fact that females who live together, work together, or are around each other a lot end up with their periods in sync.

It's a hormonal thing. You had no idea that I was out there fucking though. Stop lying."

"You can believe me or not," Faith said as I headed to our shared bathroom to wash the spit off my face, brush my teeth and take a quick shower. I felt both dirty and liberated at the same time. "I'm telling you. I was lying in my bed and my pussy started feeling like it was being hit by a jackhammer."

I giggled. "You're foolish. I'll see you in the morning."

Faith headed to her room. "Fine. Just wait and see. I bet that when I finally lose mine, you'll feel it."

In my opinion, Faith had either had too much liquor or cigga-weed at the party or she was straight up tripping. Sure, there had been times over the years where we had experienced these strange feelings when one of us was going through something. But it was ludicrous for her pussy to react to me being fucked.

Two months later, I'll be damned if I didn't feel the jackhammer working over my pussy when Faith was giving it up to Marcus. I was sitting at the kitchen table studying for a physics final, while Momma finished up the dinner dishes and all of a sudden, it felt like someone had jabbed a python up my pussy.

Oh, in case you're wondering, there isn't a damn thing special about Alabama dick. I have discovered that over the years. Don't believe the hype!

FAITH

"Oh, how I love a good dick down." I was getting dressed for APF Freak Night in our dorm room. "Hope, you need to hurry up and get dressed. We can't be late. The sorors will have a fit."

"I'm not going."

I glanced at Hope, who was sprawled out on her bed reading *One Taste* by Allison Hobbs.

"You're sitting there reading a book about a man who loves to eat pussy and you're talking about missing freak night? You better get your ass up."

"I don't have to be there every single month, Faith. It's not like all of you are going to refrain from fucking because there's one less pussy present."

I pushed her feet on the floor and sat down beside her, yanking the book out of her hands. "You know the damn rules. The sorors who plan freak night invite men based on the number of us who are expected to attend. Unless we're out of town, or home for vacation from school, we have to be there."

She glared at me with puppy dog eyes. "Don't you ever get tired of the freak nights? I mean, don't you ever want to settle down with one man and do a bunch of off-the-wall shit with him?"

I put my right palm over her forehead. She pushed it away. "This, coming from you? Soror Lick 'em Low?"

"Whatever, Ride 'em High." She sighed. "Okay, I guess that I'll go. I haven't had sex in a few days and Raheem didn't have that anaconda he was rumored to have."

I fell out laughing. "I tried to tell you that he started that lie himself to get play. Your dumb ass fell for it. Now you're another notch on his belt here at Crockett University. That's why I don't fuck around with dudes from school."

"Faith, you're always so caught up in trying to be Miss Goodie Two Shoes, ever since we were little. Then you turn around and do wilder shit than I ever could."

"I don't shit where I eat. As long as I'm keeping my business away from school, I don't ever have to worry about it spreading across campus." I got up and started putting on my black high-heel pumps. "Get up and get dressed."

"Where is freak night tonight, anyway?" Hope asked, finally

starting to move about to get dressed. I watched her shuffle through designer clothes. *Label whore!*

"It's at that cyber café over on Eighth Street."

"Oh, that's right. Soror Sweet Walls and Soror Good 'n Plenty are throwing tonight's gig. Should be interesting."

We both laughed. The two in charge for the month, whose real names were Pamela and Cornelia, gave an entire new meaning to being freaky. There was no telling what we were in for.

"I wonder what we're going to do at a cyber café," Hope added. "Should we take our laptops?"

"I can't imagine what we would need laptops for." I checked out my makeup in the mirror. "Whatever we need, they've got it covered. They didn't mention laptops. Pamela merely called with the address."

"Cool. Give me fifteen to get dressed and then we're out of here."

★★★

I thought that I had seen it all...until that month's freak night. We were indeed inside a cyber café in downtown D.C. The neighborhood was kind of deserted because Washington clears out at night, except for certain spots. The windows were tinted so people could see out but not in. Sure, there were cars driving by but no heavy foot traffic.

The place was two levels. By the time we got there, all the men were already upstairs. Pamela and Cornelia told us to get undressed; another reason why Hope did not need to be so pressed about what to wear. On freak nights, everyone ended up in their birthday suits eventually.

There were laptops on the tables where we were, along with jack rabbit vibrators, a remote control and our web cams were on. Once all of us were in place, except for the two hostesses, we went live and on each laptop appeared a fine-ass man who was upstairs. Mine looked like he was tall, even though he was seated. He was light-skinned and bald with gray eyes. He was more Hope's type than mine but I could live with it. I was sure that before the night ended, I would have meat of all flavors to toy with.

Soror Sweet Walls told us what to do downstairs while Soror Good 'n Plenty told the men what to do upstairs. Then she came to join us. Technology can be a blessing and a curse. In this case, it was definitely a blessing. The men had on vibrating thongs and now had their chairs pushed back so we could see them on our laptops. We all put the vibrators inside our pussies and positioned ourselves so they could see. Then the games began. They used the remote controls upstairs to operate the vibrators inside of us and we used our remote controls to operate their thongs. Talk about some hot shit.

There were rotating pleasure beads in the shaft of the see-thru, purple jelly dildo and a vibrating, rabbit clit vibe at the base.

"Mmmmm, this shit feels so good," I told my fuck buddy through the web cam.

"My dick is hard enough to split bricks," he said back to me through his.

His eyes were starting to roll back in his head, probably because I had increased the intensity of the vibrating action in his thong. His dick was about to burst out of it. He looked like he was hung like a mule. The thought of climbing on top of his dick in one of the chairs was exhilarating.

"What's your name?" he asked me.

"Soror Ride 'em High."

"My name is…"

"I don't want, or need to know, your name. It's against the rules," I reminded him.

He blushed. "Will you marry me?"

"I can't marry you but I can fuck the living daylights out of you." I set the remote down for a second, held two fingers to my lips and then placed a kiss on the computer screen for him. "Would you like that? You want me to give you the fuck of the century?"

"Hell yeah!" He blew me a kiss back. "You're going to make me cum!"

I had already had two orgasms. Shit, vibrators never fail! "Go ahead and bust that first nut. I'm going to handle the second one."

I glanced around the room. Sorors were working the hell out of their vibrators with one hand and the remote controls with the other. They were moaning and engaging in dirty talk with their men and I could hear the men talking shit back. A group of men walked past the front window on their way to H Street. They did not even look our way. They could not see or hear a thing. If they only knew what was going on behind those dark windows, they would have paid out the ass to be a part of the festivities.

Men were always hand selected by the hosting sorors. Despite what people said about there being a shortage of men, especially in D.C., that was not true when it came to finding available dick. No man had ever been invited back twice and we never had an issue filling up the available slots.

We *could not* have a man at a freak night more than once. It was too risky. We never held it in the same location twice either. I had no idea how Pamela and Cornelia had snagged the cyber café but I am sure it came down to cash or possibly the owner was one of the men upstairs. I did not know and I did not care. I simply wanted to get my freak on.

When I redirected my eyes back to the screen, my man was so excited that he looked like he was about to combust.

"I can't take it anymore!" he exclaimed and ripped his mule dick out of the thong right on time so I could see him shoot a load all over the screen. They had been instructed to do that and again, the shit was hot!

I also climaxed again. There was something about seeing a man lose control and shoot a load that did it for me. Some women find it nasty but someone ejaculated to get all of us here.

Hope was three tables down from me and I could not really see what she was doing, nor did I want to. Even though we're twins and both sorors of APF, there are certain visuals that I try to avoid. Sometimes it is possible, sometimes it is not. Sometimes I could feel her getting fucked, even when I was getting fucked my damn self. One day, some scientist needs to weed through that phenomenon and figure shit out.

Another thirty minutes went by as everyone else completed the game. All the men had to shoot on the screen before we could proceed. My man stayed in his seat but I could see other men walking behind him, carrying bottles of beer and telling some of the others to "hurry up so we can all get some pussy."

I was feeling impatient myself. I was ready for a good dick down. "Speed their thongs up on the remote controls. Talk nastier or something to them. Suck on your own tits to get them hot. Shit! Let's get a move on."

Soror Twister, real name, Allison, rolled her eyes at me. I could see her from eight tables down. I rolled mine back. She was probably the hold-up. *Fuckin' newbie!*

HOPE

I could sense Faith's annoyance from several tables down. Patience has never been one of her strong points. I was with her though. It was time to get down to some serious fucking. Granted, I had pulled an attitude earlier and did not really feel like transforming into Soror Lick 'em Low. But once we were there, my punany was on full alert and ready for action. I had to give it to Cornelia and Pamela; this was some off-the-chain, futuristic shit. I wonder if decades from now, when it really becomes too deadly for people to even touch each other because of STDs, if this is how people will have to get down. If it is, I don't want to be around. I can't imagine life without dick. Toys are cool but there is no substitution for the real thing.

I hear a lot of sisters talking about how they don't need a man, how they pop their own rocks with dildos and vibrators. While toys are okay from time to time, they are being delusional because the human touch—the heat—is not going to be replaced by plastic. If they expect people in the future to refrain from sex, they better set a cutoff date for fucking. Something like, all children born after 2050 have to get some immunization against getting horny. Otherwise, it will be hard as shit to prevent it. Once a person samples sex, puleeze!

I was sitting there, pondering about a world without fucking, when the final man shot his load on the screen. We could hear the men upstairs cheering, both via our laptops and because they were so damn loud. I am sure they realized that they were in for it. Hell, the cyber/remote sex was probably wilder than any fucking they had done in real life. Now, it was about to be on!

The men came stumbling down the stairs, in single file, some still holding their dripping dicks and others with wide-ass grins on their faces. They started greeting us and asking our names— our real names—and introducing themselves. We all laughed and then Soror Sweet Walls slapped one of the men across the face.

"Get down on your knees!" she yelled at him. When he stood there looking foolish, she slapped the other side of his face— harder. "Did you hear me? On your knees."

Some of the other men chuckled, while others seemed mesmerized or possibly even a little intimidated.

The one Soror Sweet Walls slapped, a medium-height, caramel brother with a fade, got down on his knees. She then threw her right leg over his shoulder and said, "Now, eat my pussy. They don't call me Soror Sweet Walls for nothing."

He started going to town on her pussy. She grabbed the back of his head and pushed his mouth deeper into her. "That's right, lick that sweet nectar. Eat it all up." She glanced at some of the other men. "On second thought, make sure you save some for the others." She started pointing the index finger of her free hand at various men. "I'm going to feed you, and you, and definitely you," she stated, pointing at the man that I had toyed with over the web cam.

Soror Good 'n Plenty came closer to them. "Now, you men have been told the rules. Don't go asking any of us our real names again or your asses are out of here. We'll simply fuck each other with the dildos and vibrators and let you all work your shit out together."

It was obvious none of them were trying to be shown the exit;

especially when they were so close to getting pussywhipped within inches of their life. Soror Good 'n Plenty added, "We don't give a shit what any of your names are. To us, you are all pieces of meat, tongue action, and vehicles for our pleasure."

She looked at Allison. "Come here, Soror Twister."

Allison moved forward, cheesing like the cat that had swallowed the canary. We all knew what was coming.

Soror Good 'n Plenty grabbed one of the other dudes; a tall, dark-skinned brother and started pushing him toward the floor. "Lie down on your back," she instructed him.

Once he had complied, she told Allison, "Do your thing, Twister. Show these pieces of meat how you roll."

Allison got down on her knees and immediately engulfed the brother's entire dick in her mouth and started gliding it in and out. Once he was hard, which did not take long, she continued to use her mouth to put a condom on his dick and then climbed on top of him. For a minute or two, she rode him with much ferocity and then came the good part. While all of the men looked on in amazement, Soror Twister rested her palms beside his shoulders and used them to brace her weight as she lifted her bottom up with her ankles locked behind her own back and started spinning on his dick.

A few of the men yelled out, "Oh, shit!" while others licked their lips and slapped each other on the arms or exchanged high-fives.

"There are plenty of Headstrong condoms in the bowls spread throughout the room," Soror Sweet Walls said, releasing the brother's head that had been locked on her pussy the entire time. "Make sure you use them and dispose of them in the boxes beside the bowls. We can't leave a sperm bank in these people's café."

All the men started grabbing for condoms. Some of them really thought that they had it going on because they were scooping up handfuls.

"Let the fuckfest begin!" Soror Good 'n Plenty said.

FAITH

He was going to make me break my rule. I never shit where I ate. In our first three years at Crockett University, I had never fucked a dude from school. Not a student, not an instructor, not an employee; no one affiliated with the place. All of that became likely to change the second I laid eyes on Kevin Nelson. Such a common name for such an uncommon man. I was walking out of the student union when I spotted him coming out of the administration building. He had to be at least six-six and he had a lot of body; good body.

He was dark-skinned and had dreadlocks that hung to about the middle of his back. Even across the yard, I could see his eyes. Those eyes. Eyes that were slightly slanted and were an unusual shade of brown. If I had to assign a color to his eyes, I guess that sienna would have to do. He was walking with Mr. Jones, the vice president of the university. I stood frozen as I watched them make their way in my direction.

"Hello, Faith," Mr. Jones said as they passed me.

I smiled slightly but could not manage to get a word out. Kevin—whose name I did not even know at that point—winked at me and grinned.

They entered the student union and disappeared into the mass of students. After I finally gathered my composure, I glanced at the time on my cell phone and realized that I was late for class.

"Shit!" I said to no one in particular. I hesitated for a brief moment before heading back into the student union. I could miss a day of class but I could not take the chance of never seeing that man again. I had to find out more about him.

I found the two of them sitting at a table in the cafeteria. All of the students and staff passing by were on their best behavior, speaking as they walked by. Mr. Jones was a nice man and everyone liked him ten times more than the university president, Mrs. Walker. He was a widower and all of his kids were grown. Yet and still, he had the swagger and demeanor of a man half his age. Some of the females on campus used to tease about giving him a run for his money in the bedroom. They all knew that he would never do such a thing though. The man had morals.

As I approached their table, I tried to think of an excuse to say something.

"Mr. Jones." I stood there and tried to make eye contact with him, but I really wanted to stare his table mate down. "Can I ask you a question?"

"Sure, Faith." Mr. Jones put his water glass down. "I spoke to you outside but your mind must have been in another place."

"Oh, I'm so sorry." I sighed. "I've been kind of overwhelmed; this being the beginning of my senior year and all."

Mr. Jones chuckled. "It's been a long road but it's almost over. You've got a bright future ahead of you; both you and your sister."

"Thanks."

"So what can I help you with today, Faith?"

My mind started racing. "I was wondering if there is any way you can help me get an internship. I have some great possibilities but a letter of recommendation from you would put me way ahead of the other candidates. Competition is fierce for most of the positions."

"Sure! It would be my honor," he replied. "Chemical engineering major, right?"

"You got it!"

"Sometimes, I get the two of you mixed up. Your sister's major is journalism."

"It's amazing how you can remember so much about all the students on campus, Mr. Jones."

"I try but I must confess that I don't have a photographic memory when it comes to all the students. Being that you are the only set of twins currently on campus, it makes the two of you stand out."

"Twins?" my future husband asked. "Cool!"

Mr. Jones cleared his throat. "My apologies. How rude must I seem today? Faith Andrews, this is Kevin Nelson. Kevin is our new chief financial officer."

He stood up and shook my hand. He was a tree! "Nice to meet you, Ms. Andrews."

"Ditto," I replied. "Chief financial officer, huh? I guess that means that you are the one who will make sure the school doesn't go belly up."

He winked at me again as he sat back down. "That will never happen on my watch."

I remained still for another moment before I realized that I was making a fool of myself. They were apparently waiting for me to leave so they could continue their conversation.

"Is there anything else, Faith?" Mr. Jones asked.

"No, that's all," I said.

"I can have the letter of recommendation for you by Monday. Will that suffice?"

"That's absolutely perfect!" *Just like the fine man sitting across from you*, I thought.

"Take care," Kevin said.

"You, too."

I turned and walked slowly away. My panties were soaking wet. I swear that I had an orgasm, from merely looking at the man.

★★★

For the next few days, I was a madwoman. I was searching the Internet trying to find out anything I could about Kevin Nelson. His photo and brief bio were on the university site but that was not enough for me. It stated that he was originally from Tennessee and had gone to college in Maine. *Maine! Did they even have black people in Maine?*

Monday could not get here fast enough for me. Hope was out of town for the weekend. She decided to ride with one of our dorm mates, Janice, to Hampton University to see her boyfriend. Hope was not slick. I knew that she had her eye on some dude at the same school but she denied it. My sister was not about to spend five seconds as the third wheel, rather less a couple of days. She craved attention way too much. That was one of the reasons she was such a label whore.

I lurked around the dorm that weekend, constantly masturbating and fantasizing about Kevin. I had no clue about his situation. He could have been married, shacking up, or even gay. None of that changed the fact that he was heavy on my mind. I had invented such a buildup in my mind about the man that he would have to be the fuck of the century to live up to it.

I did not mention my infatuation to Hope. She would have been relentless in her teasing. I was always the calm and collected twin. There was never a man that I could not take or leave… until then.

★★★

On Monday, I waited until about eleven a.m. before I headed over to the administration building. I had attended my two morning classes and was freed up until around two. I went to Mr. Jones' office first and his secretary handed me a brown clasp envelope with the letter of recommendation in it. When I got back out into the hallway, I paced back and forth for a couple of minutes before I sucked in a deep breath and headed to the other end to Kevin's office.

The outer office was empty. His secretary must have stepped out. Good, because I did not really have a plan of action in place and might have sounded like a fool or stuttered or something. I inched my way toward the open door to his inner office and I could hear him on the phone.

I started to back away but then I heard him say, "Yes? Can I help you?"

He must have seen my shadow. *Shit!*

I stepped forward and waved, like a silly little schoolgirl waving to her father on the first day of kindergarten as he drove away in the family station wagon.

He had the receiver of the phone covered up with one hand. "I'll be right with you, Faith."

Damn, he remembers my name! I thought before blushing.

He motioned me toward one of the leather wing chairs on the visitors' side of his desk. I sat down and crossed my legs. I had spent a lot of time making sure that my skin was silky smooth and had even put on one of Hope's designer casual dresses. Might as well make some good use out of her clothes, instead of her wasting them on little boys.

"How about next Wednesday at seven?" he inquired of someone on the phone. "We can meet at Posh." He paused. "Yes, right over on Eleventh Street, across from the Hyatt." He winked at me. I melted. "Great. See you then, Gary."

He hung up. "Sorry about that. Gary's a friend from college. We haven't seen each other in ages and he's in town for a few weeks on a contract job."

"I should be the one apologizing. I interrupted your phone conversation."

We sat there, grinning at each other, speaking with our eyes instead of with words. I could tell he wanted me. No, sir, this was not a gay man in front of me.

"So what brings you here?" he asked. "I must admit, I cannot imagine a more pleasant interruption."

"Not to get into your business, but Posh is a great restaurant. Have you tried their shrimp and grits?"

"No, I haven't. I usually get the salmon but since you suggested it, I will definitely be getting that when I meet Gary."

I did not want to be embarrassed by him having to ask me again why I was there, and I could not come up with anything that made sense...other than the truth. Shit, I was Soror Ride 'em High and I was acting like a virgin.

"Mr. Nelson, um..."

"Kevin. Call me Kevin, Faith."

"Kevin, can I be honest with you?"

He chuckled. "I believe most people prefer honesty over deception."

I laughed uneasily.

"What's on your mind, young lady?"

When he called me "young lady," I was thrown for a loop. Did the comment mean that he thought of me as a child?

"I'm not that young," I informed him. "I'm a senior. I'll be twenty-two in a few months."

"And I'll be forty-five in March," he said. "Since I'm more than twice your age, that would make you young in my eyes."

"What about in your bed?" I blurted out.

A wide grin spread across his face.

I hopped up out of the seat. "I shouldn't have said that. I was out of line. Please pretend like it never happened."

Before I could get to the door, he reached over me and closed it. "Don't run off," he whispered as he towered over me. "What if I don't want to pretend it never happened?"

I turned and looked up at him—way up at him. "How tall are you, Kevin?"

"Six-eight."

"Damn!"

"How tall are you?" he asked me.

"Five-two."

"I like short women. They are easier to toss around and assume the position."

I ran my fingers over his belt buckle and then up his chest.

"And what position might that be?"

"Um, let's see. There's the pile driver, the sitting bull, the twister, the deep impact, the mirror of pleasure and the bumper cars."

"Shit, you sound like you're on top of your game."

"There's no substitute for experience," he reminded me.

"So they say." I glanced at the doorknob. "Does this thing lock?" I asked.

He locked the door and took a step back. "What's on your mind?"

"I realize that you're more experienced than me." I decided

to give him credit; even though that was debatable. He may have been much older but not many women my age were members of Alpha Phi Fuckem. I was intrigued by the positions he mentioned and definitely planned to look those bad boys up as soon as I got back to my dorm. "But," I continued, "I know a trick or two myself."

"Really?"

"Oh, yes." I started unbuckling his belt. "I bet you have a monstrosity in your pants."

"It's bigger than most; surely smaller than some." Kevin ran his fingers through my hair. "You want to see it?"

"I'm *going* to see it." I got his belt undone and then I started working on the button of his pants and the zipper. "And then I'm going to taste it."

"I taste good," he informed me.

"Let me be the judge of that."

When I lowered his pants and black boxers, I was pleasantly surprised. I knew his dick would be living large but it was also beautiful…if there could ever be such a thing as a beautiful dick.

"Take off your shoes and get your pants all the way off," I told him.

"My secretary will be back in about thirty minutes."

"Trust, you could never handle thirty minutes of head from me." I giggled. "I suck a mean dick."

The fact that he was tall made it so much easier for me to jackhammer his ass.

I got down on the floor and sat on my behind with my knees up, then scooted back toward him, facing away from him. "Spread your legs, Kevin," I instructed him.

Once he did, I leaned my head back and pulled his semi-hard

dick into my mouth. He immediately got the point and started flexing his legs, moving up and down until we both caught a rhythm. My nose was buried in his balls and I inhaled his scent. Damn, a beautiful dick and sweet balls. I was dick-whipped and he hadn't even fucked me yet.

I used one hand to guide his dick in and out of my mouth and the other to play with his anus. He had no problem with it, so I stuck my index finger inside and started moving it back and forth.

"Oh shit!" he said, almost in a whimper. "You're going to make me cum!"

I almost choked as I held back a laugh. Imagine, he had thought thirty minutes would not be enough time for me to get him off. I took his dick out for a minute and started pulling on his testicles with my mouth, popping them in and out of my cheeks like gumballs. When he moaned and shivered, I returned to the dick.

Three or four minutes later, he was shooting a full load. I moved away right on time because a swallower I was not. Not unless I was in a monogamous relationship and that had never really happened. His semen splattered all over the carpet and he collapsed back in a chair.

I got on my knees and licked the sides of his dick as he tried to regain his composure. He started running his fingers through my hair again.

"That was a nice appetizer," I whispered. "When can I enjoy the main course?"

"Whenever you want," he replied. "But not here. What we did was a foolish, foolish thing."

"Did you enjoy it?" I made eye contact with him while I played with the remaining sperm on the tip of his dick with my fingers.

"I loved it!"

"Then what's done is done." I got up. "But I agree. We can't fuck in here." I took a sticky note off his desk and grabbed a pen and wrote down my cell number. "Here's my number. Call me tonight, if that's cool."

"What time tonight?" Kevin asked.

"I have to do a study lab but I'm free any time after ten."

"Forget about calling you. Let's make plans now."

I blushed. I couldn't wait to lay it on him. "Sure."

"Meet me at eleven, in front of the library. I'll be in a black Mercedes."

I caressed his fine-ass face and then kissed him on the forehead. "Eleven. Library. Black Mercedes. Big black dick. Got it."

He laughed. "You are something else."

"Kevin, you have not seen a damn thing yet. I'm going to be ready for you tonight. Looking good. Smelling good. I want to know what that damn deep impact is all about. If it is anywhere near as catastrophic as the movie, I might not be able to walk tomorrow."

He grinned and slapped me on the ass as I walked toward the door.

"Shit, I may be the one not able to walk tomorrow," he said.

I decided to wink at him for a change as I exited the door. I was anxious to see what his dick action was really like. Eleven o'clock could not get there fast enough for me.

HOPE

Faith was up to something. I had no idea what it was, and that was the part that disturbed me. She was obviously fucking someone but it was some sort of top secret, covert type of shit. She never said she was fucking but, like always, I could feel it in my cooch, just like she knew when I was getting busy.

Whoever the dude was, my twin was smiling, and I had not seen her so damn happy in a long time. She would leave out late at night and come back way over in the morning, claiming to have been pulling all-nighters in the engineering building. Granted, chemical engineering was no major to laugh at but I was nobody's fool. I could not get too mad. I was fucking Nick at Hampton and had not told Faith. There was no reasoning behind it. Simply never felt like discussing it. I'm sure she knew that I was not making road trips with Janice for no reason. Janice and I were cool but not that damn cool. There was no way that I was going to ride in a car for hours and not get some dick when I arrived.

★★★

I was at Dante's Peak one night, chilling at the bar, when the strangest—most wonderful—thing happened. This tall, handsome drink of water walked up behind me, grabbed me around the waist and whispered, "I want you."

I turned around and stared at him. He winked and I grinned. He was a giant. Fine as shit.

"Do I know you?" I asked. There was no chance of my ever forgetting his face…or his body.

He chuckled. Then he repeated himself and said, "I want you."

"Well, I might want you, too." I decided to play along. My pussy was pulsating to the bass of the music and I was down for some freaky business. It had been a minute since I had engaged in a one-night stand, outside of APF freak nights, of course.

He took my hand and led me from the bar upstairs to the VIP section where they had private alcoves with booths in them.

"I missed you," he said to me before burying his tongue in my mouth.

Shit, what was a girl to do, except reciprocate?

We kissed for a few moments. His tongue was long and thick and I wondered what it would feel like buried inside my pussy. Closed mouths don't get fed. In that particular case, eaten, so I went for it.

I ended the kiss, gazed into his eyes, and said, "Lick my pussy."

People were walking past the booth but they either did not notice or did not care. Everyone knew that Dante's Peak was a bona fide fuck spot.

"Gladly," he replied.

I decided to get super freaky and pulled my dress up around my waist, then sat down on the bench in the booth, lay back and raised my legs all the way up so that my ankles were on either side of my head. He got on his knees behind me and held my ass up with one hand and moved the crotch of my red lace thongs to the side with the other one. Then he commenced to eating his pie in the sky. Let's just say the brother had a serious sweet tooth.

I could see people staring then. Stopping in their tracks and gazing on in amazement. There we were, with my pussy up in the air and him going to town on it. My kind of man.

Finally a bouncer came over to the booth and told us we had to "stop that shit or get out."

We did both. Before ten minutes had expired, we were fucking like crazy in his black Mercedes. "I've missed you," he whispered to me again.

I eased off of riding him for a second and gazed into his eyes. "Why do you keep saying that?"

"Because I have missed you, Faith."

When he said Faith's name, my mouth fell open. He started kissing me on my neck and driving his dick up into me further and further. I was speechless.

I realize that I should have stopped right then. I should have told him that I was really Hope and that there had been a serious mistake. But then what? What was I supposed to do? Go back to the dorm and tell my twin sister that I had fucked her man? That he had eaten me out in a nightclub in front of a bunch of people? Tell him that I was not Faith and let him go tell her that I played some sort of trick on him? I knew nothing about the character of this man. All I knew is that he could damn near suck the ovaries out of a pussy and he had a big dick. But he seemed to be sincere about missing my sister.

All I could think was *damn, damn, damn,* and the worst part was that I finished fucking him in his car...and it felt good. Afterward, I was about to get out of the car but he grabbed my wrist.

"I'll take you back to the dorm."

"I have the Hummer," I said.

"Oh, okay, I thought your sister drove it most of the time."

I stared at him. "She does...most of the time, but I have it tonight."

"I didn't realize you hung out here. Or that you went clubbing at all."

Great! Now he wanted to play Twenty Questions!

I did not respond. Just shrugged. "I'll catch you later."

"When?" he asked.

"Call me tomorrow." Common sense told me that he had Faith's number since he knew so much about me cruising in the SUV and her being a dorm rat.

"You need a ride to your vehicle?"

"No, I'm straight," I said.

I got out and walked away swiftly. I could feel his eyes on my back. All I could do from that point was pray for a miracle. That he would not mention what happened that night in some form of remembrance with Faith, about the bomb-ass oral sex in the club and the sex in the car. If he had been fucking my sister, how could he not tell the difference? Granted, we looked alike, we could tell when the other was fucking, but was it possible for us to have the same exact pussy? For us to taste the same? The truly fucked-up part was that I didn't even know the man's name.

FAITH

Kevin and I had been seeing each other for about two months, unbeknownst to anyone else. I planned to keep it that way. I was not ashamed of the fact that we were dating. It was more like I had no idea where it was headed. He had two sons around my age. One was in the Navy and married with two children and the other one was working on his masters in California. He had divorced their mother seven years into the marriage but had remained a devoted father. She had apparently cheated on him with one of his best friends and was also suffering from manic depression. Of course, all of this was his side of the story. There are always the proverbial three sides: his side, her side and the truth.

I did know that he talked to his sons. They would call him at various times when we were together. Their names were Decha and Geechi, as his ex-wife was African and had chosen the names. He would always tell either one that he loved them before they got off the phone. That in itself earned him brownie points with me. Any man who could express love so openly and freely to two other grown men would surely express it daily to the love of his life. Part of me wanted to be that love. The other part, I had to admit, was a tiny bit apprehensive about what my parents would think. Kevin was only three years younger than our father. Even though I was a grown-ass woman, Daddy would surely label Kevin as a pedophile and accuse him of taking advantage of his innocent daughter. I was as far from innocent as they came.

Kevin would often cook for me at his house. He had a quaint little brick house on Capitol Hill with a great view of many D.C. landmarks. Often we would walk around the Reflecting Pool, holding hands and talking about life. There was much wisdom to be gained from him and I could appreciate that. What I appreciated even more was the way he laid his hands on me. Sex with Kevin was nothing short of incredible. Sometimes he was inside of me within minutes and other times he would take his time with me, and slowly satisfy and pay attention to every inch of my being.

I loved the way he would gaze into my eyes whenever we were in a face-to-face position. And when I could not see him, he would always whisper sweet nothings in my ear or caress my shoulders while he fucked me with much intensity from behind. He had shown me all those positions that he mentioned that first day in his office and then some. What was really silly—and I guess showed my age—was that often a streak of jealousy would overcome me when he worked me over with such expertise. I often wondered who else he had done such things with. His wife? Or tons of women? It should not have mattered, I realized, because he was with me now. Even if it turned out to be a temporary thing, I would have been pleased if I could only be with him for my last year in college.

But then the craziest thing happened. He asked me a question.

"So, if we get married, how many kids do you want?"

I was sitting at his kitchen counter, finishing up a class assignment on my laptop, when he said it. He was sautéeing some shrimp, chicken and vegetables in a wok. Kevin was this incredible cook.

I looked up at him for a few seconds and then continued to type.

"Aren't you going to answer me?"

"Are your sons tall?" I asked, instead of answering.

"What?"

"Are your sons tall? I've never asked you that. I've seen their baby pictures but you don't have any current ones around the house."

Kevin looked irritated. "Yes, my sons are tall. Geechi is six-five and Decha is six-seven."

"Wow! I would hate to be a man with a Napoleon complex when the three of you walk into a room."

Kevin chuckled and finished up the food, unplugging the wok and taking two plates out of the cabinet. As he distributed the great-smelling concoction evenly, he said, "I guess that made you uneasy. My question."

"No, not at all. You kind of took me off guard." I took a sip of the Chardonnay that I had grown used to drinking over his house. "I've never really given much thought to having kids. I do want them…someday. I need to get my career together first.

Hell, I need to get my degree first." I got up from the stool and walked over to him, placing my hands around his waist. My head only came to the middle of his shoulder blades so I buried my nose into his back. His Issey Miyake cologne invaded my senses and I wanted to lick him all over like a lollipop. "Do you have any idea how much I love sucking your big, juicy dick, Kevin?"

He grabbed my left hand and lifted it to his mouth, kissing the tips of my fingers gently. "No, but tell me. Tell me how much you love sucking my dick."

"I could suck your dick for breakfast, lunch and dinner. I could suck it for a midnight snack, to get rid of a toothache, to cure a headache. There is something magical about your dick."

"Magical?" He turned, looked down at me, and blushed.

"Yes, you know, magic is technically any type of human ability to predict or control the natural world, such as people, events, and objects."

"Is that right, Faith?"

"Yes." I started rubbing him to hardness through his pants. "Since you control me with your dick, then you must be practicing some sort of sorcery on me or something."

He stunned me by pushing me away from him slightly. "Is my dick really the only thing you're interested in? If all you want is a fuck partner, or a cut buddy like the younger generation calls it, I'm not interested."

"I'm sorry, Kevin. I didn't mean to come off that way," I said apologetically. "I thought that was all I was to you...until you asked me about kids."

"What would make you think that, considering how much time we spend together?"

I shrugged. "Assumptions. The way that I came onto you in

your office and started gulping down your dick in less than five minutes. I never thought you would take me seriously."

"Well, I take what we are doing very seriously." He pulled me back to him, leaned down, and kissed me passionately, then added, "You make me feel very special. You make me feel like the man that I've always wanted to be."

I was blown away. "In what way?"

"In, oh, so many ways." He gazed into my eyes and caressed the back of my neck. "Even though I've had my share of women, I can't lie about that, you have brought something alive in me that no one else has. Sometimes, it even frightens me."

I slapped him playfully on the chest. "Big men like you don't get frightened."

"A man's height doesn't determine the size of his heart. Some men my size don't even have a heart, and some men your size have gigantic ones."

"Never thought of it that way."

"My heart is filled with so much emotion right now."

At that very moment, I was ready to do practically anything for Kevin. There was something about him, from the first second that I laid eyes on him. To top it all off, he had the nerve to not only be fine, but kindhearted, sensual, and now apparently capable of deep feelings.

"I tell you what," I said to him. "Why don't we heat up the dinner a little bit later so we can have a quick appetizer in the bedroom first?"

He flashed that sexy-ass grin of his again. "Why the bedroom?"

I giggled. "Why indeed."

We started working each other's clothes off and before the Will Downing CD had slipped over to the next track, Kevin was seated on one of the dining room chairs with a Headstrong condom on and I was facing away from him, giving him a good old-fashioned lap dance with his dick buried inside of me.

"You feel so damn good!" I exclaimed.

He grabbed me by the shoulders and kissed the middle of my spine as we ground our way into a frenzy. We both exploded and I collapsed back onto his strong chest.

"Faith, I think I love you," he whispered in my ear. Before I could respond, he said, "Shh, don't say anything. I don't want you to say something you don't mean."

"But…"

"But nothing. Rarely do two people reach the same point at the same time. I am confident that you'll get there. I can wait."

I climbed off of him and stood. He started suckling on my breasts as he remained in the chair. I ran my fingers through his dreads.

"Kevin, my sister and I have to go home in a couple of days for Thanksgiving but when I get back, I'd really like for us to sit down and have a serious conversation about this thing that we're doing."

He kept nipping hungrily at my breasts. That shit turned me on so much.

"Do you hear me, Kevin?"

"I hear you, baby." He looked me in the eyes. "I hear you and I agree. But will I see you again before you leave?"

"It would have to be a quickie."

He reached around with both hands and grabbed my ass cheeks. "I love a quickie every now and then."

"The way you're devouring my breasts, I think it's time to eat dinner."

We both fell out laughing and spent the rest of the evening lying naked on his living room floor, eating dinner and enjoying each other's bodies.

HOPE

"Raheem, I really can't see you tonight." I was walking across campus, trying to get away from the fool. "I have plans."

"Oh, come on, Hope." He grabbed my elbow and spun me around, almost causing me to drop my stack of books. Faith was right about Raheem. He was not a gentleman at all. He never offered to carry my books for me. "Break a brother off with a little something-something before we all head home for Thanksgiving."

"How many times do I have to tell you that I am not available tonight?"

"Call that other Negro and tell him you're going to be with a real man."

I smirked. "What makes you assume this has anything to do with another dude? My sister and I have to take care of something before we drive to Atlanta. It's as simple as fucking that." I started walking away from him. "Stop pressuring me. We don't even get down like that. Friends with benefits doesn't mean you get to control my ass."

"No, but I love your ass control," he said, trying to make a joke.

"I bet you do."

He grabbed me from behind, irritating me even more. "I love what you do with your ass, your pussy, and for damn sure, your mouth."

I was tempted to blurt out, "That's why they call me Soror Lick 'em Low," but I couldn't. Sometimes I hated having to be so secretive about Alpha Phi Fuckem.

Instead, I smacked my lips and pushed him off of me. "Don't you have class clear across campus in ten minutes?" I asked him.

"Yeah," Raheem replied, "but I'd rather take you to class, in my dorm room. I have something I want to teach you."

"You start skipping class and your grades will drop, and there goes your football scholarship. Even my bomb-ass pussy isn't worth all that. My pussy isn't going to pay your bills after graduation."

Raheem chuckled. "You know, sometimes you make a lot of sense, Hope."

"Shit, I make sense all the time." I gave him a quick peck on the cheek. "Now go to class and stop acting like my man. We'll work something out next week, when we both get back."

"I'm going to hold you to that shit, baby."

He finally started walking off; *thank goodness*. I liked fucking. No, I loved fucking, but I was not trying to be in love. That shit was for the birds. Even at such a young age, I had already determined that most men were full of shit and only out for sex. The days of giving real love and having it reciprocated were over.

I was standing there, shaking my head and thinking about how most women have accepted the fact that they are going to share dick for the rest of their lives, when a black Mercedes pulled up beside me on the curb. Not just any black Mercedes though. HIS black Mercedes.

He rolled down the passenger side window. "Get in, Faith."

"I...I..." I could not get more than that out.

He started looking around in all directions. "Hurry up, before someone sees us."

My mind was going in one direction but my feet started moving toward his car. He reached over with his long arm and pushed the door open. Once I had climbed in, he rolled the window back up and took off from the curb with a jerk.

"Put your seatbelt on," he instructed me. "Can't have anything happen to my precious cargo."

He grinned at me and started rubbing my thigh. I had on winter tights and a skirt with a sweater.

"Where are we going?" I asked, recognizing that I had less than zero business in his vehicle.

"I know you said that we'd have to have a quickie if I saw you before you left, but we can't do it here. If Mr. Jones saw us, I might get fired."

When he mentioned the vice president of the university and used the word "fired," things came together quickly. *He worked at Crockett University, and Faith was fucking him!* That was so against her rules. No wonder she had never mentioned it to me. She was constantly riding me about steering away from men at school, but she had taken her shit to another level. Slick ass!

"So where are we going?" I asked again.

"A friend of mine has a spot about a mile away. He left me the key. We can be in and out in an hour."

"Oh," was my only response.

"I'm surprised to see you. I thought you had class."

Faith was indeed in class. "The teacher cancelled. Family emergency."

He laughed. "More like wanting to take an extra day or two off for the holiday, more than likely. I'm not sure who is slicker around here. The students or the staff."

"True."

Now a normal person would have told him the truth. That I was really Hope and that he had made a mistake. I had gotten away with fucking him the first time and that should have taught me a lesson. Plus, it was an honest misunderstanding. This time I was about to do something downright dirty—nasty and skank even. Even during freak nights with our sorors, Faith and I never fucked the same men. There was a silent code of ethics between my twin and me.

But there was something about this man—whose name I did not even know—whose dick I had craved since the last time it had been buried inside of me—that made my common sense evaporate. I wanted to fuck him again, but I did not want to get caught.

"I need to be back by seven," I said. "I need to go somewhere."

"You told me that already." He moved his hand further up my thigh, closer to my flaming hot pussy. "I'll have you back way beforehand. I promise. It will be quick, but good."

"It's always good," I said, settling into the role of Faith and acting like I fucked the man on the regular. "You know how to work magic all over my body."

He turned serious on me. I could hear it in his voice. "I meant what I said the other day. I would really like to take this relationship further. I hope that I didn't scare you when I asked if you wanted kids."

Damn! It's like that! I thought to myself. *Get out of the car, Hope! Get out right now!*

When I did not respond, he added, "I'm not ashamed of our relationship. You're not a minor and while some people might have an issue with it, that's on them. Sure, we can't fuck in my office anymore because they would get rid of me; CFO or not. But that has nothing to do with the way I feel for you."

So he was the chief financial officer. I remembered that the position had been open during the second half of our junior year. Something about misappropriation of funds or possible embezzlement. I rarely made it over to the administration building for any reason, so that explained why I had never seen him. Hell, I did not even know how Faith could have met him. Obviously, she had seen the inside of his office because he said they couldn't fuck in there *anymore*.

"Faith?"

"I'm sorry," I said, snapping out of my trance and gazing into his eyes. "I was thinking about something."

"About me?" He lifted my left hand to his mouth and kissed it. "About us?"

"Yes, about us."

I shifted toward him and was about to come clean when he suddenly announced, "Here we are. He lives on the second floor."

He parallel parked and within seconds was opening the door on my side. He took me by the hand and led me to the front of the building. Once inside, we walked up the steps to the second floor and stopped in front of apartment 2-D. There was a key on top of the doorframe.

"My man," he said. "Howard never lets a brother down."

My mind went into overdrive. Was he using this Howard's apartment as some sort of love nest near campus? Did he bring a bunch of coeds over here for easy access during the workday? Was he playing my sister?

It seems crazy, looking back at it. For me to be worried about what he was doing when I was the one about to fuck my twin's man—for the second time.

"Come on in." He walked inside and turned on a lamp since the shades were drawn. "Make yourself at home."

"Thanks." I shut the door behind me and stood in the foyer. "You know, maybe we should get back. This isn't such a good idea."

He sat down on the sofa and stared at me, as I remained half-way in the shadows. "What isn't such a good idea? Making love?"

"Your friend might come home."

"No, he's not coming home until tonight. He's in Virginia Beach on business." He started rubbing his crotch and licking his lips. "He left the key. He knows we're here."

"But if you thought that I would be tied up in class, why did you even ask him to leave a key?"

"Huh?"

There was a flicker of concern in his eyes.

"Why did you ask for a key if you didn't expect to see me today? Were you planning on bringing someone else here? Have you brought someone else here before?"

"No, I was not planning on bringing someone else, and no, I have not. I asked for the key because of wishful thinking. You said that we might be able to have a quickie and I wanted to increase the possibility of that. Is that a crime?"

I did not respond.

"Faith, are you okay? You're not acting like yourself."

That's because I'm not Faith!

"I'm fine." I moved into the living area. "Just a little on edge. It's not like me to do these types of things. Being in someone else's place like this."

"But it is like you to be eaten out inside a club," he said, then chuckled, referring to what had occurred at Dante's Peak.

Shit! You should see me in action during a freak night!

"This quickie is turning into a long conversation." He grinned at me. "Come over here and get your dick."

Something came over me—and my pussy. "My dick, huh?" I walked over to him, pulling my sweater over my head at the same time. "I like the sound of that."

"You like the taste of it, too." His voice seeped with confidence. Faith must have been damn near sucking his dick down to the bone, the way he was grinning. "Get down here and do your thing, girl."

"Only if you do me, too." I turned around and lifted my skirt and started wiggling my ass in his face. He slapped me on the buttocks and then started yanking at my tights, trying to pull them down. "Wait, let me take off my boots."

Before I could even sit down on the sofa good, he was pulling my boots off and then started ripping at my tights with his teeth. He was on an animalistic tip—and I loved it!

Once we were both naked, I climbed on top of him and assumed the position—69, that is—and we went to town on each other. That was my first time sucking his dick but obviously Faith had done it a bunch of times. I was determined to live up to my name—Soror Lick 'em Low. First, I did the Hoover method on him. I closed my mouth around his humongous dick, creating a seal, and then sucked some of the air out of my mouth. I used my tongue as I moved my head up and down, creating the perfect amount of pressure. Over the years I had learned to gauge the exact pressure points to turn a man out. He was losing it as I worked his dick over like the master that I was.

That did not prevent him from dining on my pussy like it was his last meal on Earth. I am telling you, that man had a magical tongue. I had had my pussy eaten countless times but he took the prize. We moaned and licked and sucked for what seemed like hours, but it was really only about twenty minutes. Then he pushed me gently off of him and led me to the bedroom.

His friend's bedroom was fly as all get out. Mirrors on the ceiling, a black lacquer king-sized waterbed, and silk sheets, and a faux leopard fur comforter. For a second, I wondered if the sheets were clean and then I snapped back to reality. I was a member of APF, after all, and the way we got down at freak nights, clean sheets were the last concern.

Kevin put on a Headstrong condom, and then lay on the bed. I placed my feet on both sides of his waist and started riding him like a cowgirl. It was incredible. You have to be creative when you fuck extremely tall men. There are advantages—like big dicks—and disadvantages—like not being able to do a lot of the common positions. You have to be creative and creative we were for the rest of the afternoon.

When he dropped me back off on campus, he tried to insist that he pull up in front of the dorm. I quickly came up with an excuse not to.

"Please drop me off in front of the engineering building," I said.

"How come? You're done with class for the day, right?"

"Yes, but you know that was *supposed* to be a quickie, and it turned into a marathon."

He flashed his sexy grin at me. "What does that have to do with dropping you off in front of the engineering building?"

"I need to finish up one last experiment before I leave for Thanksgiving break."

"What type of experiment?"

I laughed nervously. I was a journalism major and did not know a damn thing about chemical engineering—Faith's major—rather less about experiments.

"You sure are nosey," I said jokingly. "You better watch out before I experiment on your ass."

"Stay away from my ass, except for that thing you do with your finger, but you're welcome to experiment on my dick any time you like."

He pulled his car up to the front of the building and stopped as I wondered what Faith had been doing to his anus with her finger. He was about to get out and walk around to open my door.

"That's okay," I said. "We don't need to give people something to talk about."

"Like I told you earlier, Faith. I'm not ashamed of our relationship. I can't wait to take it further."

My stomach suddenly tied up in knots. I had every reason under the sun to be ashamed of myself—and I was. At least part of me was. The other part was walking on clouds, after having experienced some of the most gratified fucking in my life.

"I really have to go," I told Kevin.

He leaned over and slid his tongue in my mouth for a brief moment. "I'm going to miss you while you're gone."

"It's only for a few days."

"When you get back, I'll cook you another dinner. We almost set my place on fire after the one the other night."

He winked at me and, of course, I was clueless about what he meant.

"That sounds nice." I opened the door to get out. "Take care."

Kevin grabbed my hand and squeezed it. "You don't have to say it back but I want you to know that I love you, Faith. One day, you'll love me back. I'm determined to make that happen."

My mouth flew open but no words came out.

He released my hand. "I'll let you go. Call me when you get to Atlanta, to let me know you got there safely."

"Sure," I said and finished getting out.

My legs were cold because my tights had been ruined so my legs were bare. I was walking up the steps to the building when Kevin rolled down his window.

"Hey, silly, I said call me when you get to Atlanta. Not now."

"Huh?" I asked.

"Your cell phone is calling me by mistake."

I almost fainted. Then I pretended to fumble through my purse, looking for my phone. "Oh, sorry."

He chuckled and pulled off.

By the time I retrieved my phone, Faith's name was on my screen. It was vibrating from her call.

"Faith?" I said, after flipping it open.

"Hope, where the hell are you?" she blared into the phone.

"Um, I'm on my way back to the dorm. I just left the journalism building," I lied. "Why?"

"Why? Why do you think?" she said with much disdain. "You need to finish packing and you also need to get ready for tonight."

"I don't need to pack much. Hell, we're going home. Both of us have a shitload of clothes in Atlanta."

Faith laughed. "But label whores always carry a bunch of shit on trips; even when it makes no sense."

"Whatever, hooker," I said, then giggled. "I'll be there in a few."

After I flipped my phone closed, I sat down on the steps of the engineering building and reflected on the hot ghetto mess that I had gotten myself into. I tried to convince myself that I was not the only guilty party. Kevin had to realize, even if it was subconsciously, that he was not fucking Faith when he was fucking me. Was it even possible for a man not to be able to tell the difference? Even with twins?

I tried to make sense of it all but I know that I was wrong—all by myself. Kevin loved Faith and there I was, fucking him like it was no big deal.

As if things could not get worse, my phone rang again. It was our mother. Talk about adding insult to injury. I felt even guiltier as she told me how excited she was about us coming home for Thanksgiving. I was going to have to go to my parents' house, break bread, and pretend like I had not been giving up my pussy out of both sides of my drawers to my sister's man.

FAITH

Hope came into our dorm room looking like she had walked through a hurricane.

"Damn!" I exclaimed. "What the hell happened to you?"

"What?" she asked, like she did not already know her appearance was crazy.

I waved her off. "Never mind. Please hurry up and take a shower so we can get going. We can't be late."

"You can go ahead in front of me."

"No, I can't and you know it. Tonight is our responsibility and we have to be on point with our shit."

"I'm surprised you're still so much into freak night," Hope said.

I was lacing up my black leather boots and stopped to glance up at her from my bed. "Why are you surprised?"

She stared at me, and then sighed. "No reason." She shrugged. "You seem a little preoccupied lately and I thought the entire Alpha Phi Fuckem thing might have taken a back seat in your life."

I finished with my boots and stood up to put on my sweater.

"Hope, I'll admit that as we approach graduation, things have become more complex in my life. I'm sure the same is true for you." She shrugged again. "We are about to embark on another stretch of our lives. Going out here; becoming career women; settling down with the men of our dreams."

She raised an eyebrow. "Oh, have you met the man of your dreams, Faith?"

I hesitated, then answered, "No, I don't think so, but you never know. I may have already met him and you may have already met yours."

Hope snickered. "I *definitely* haven't met mine. But who's tickling your fancy these days, Sis?"

"No one in particular."

I could not tell if Hope knew that I was lying. It was almost as if she sensed something, which was not uncommon when it came to us. I was of the belief that she had been off somewhere fucking all afternoon but I did not care; especially if she was still doing that asshole Raheem. I wondered if she had heard something about Kevin and me, but who would have said something? No one really knew anything. We had been so careful.

"Are you going to wash your ass or what?" I asked her. "It's smelling kind of *fishy* up in here."

"Stop worrying about my coochie, tramp."

We both laughed as Hope grabbed her shower cap and headed into the bathroom to shower.

★★★

An hour later we were standing inside the ice rink that Hope and I had rented out for the night. The other sorors were trickling in, excited about what we had in store for the night. Eyes lit up as they noticed the swing stands scattered all over the ice. There was a sex swing attached to each one. The men were in one of the locker rooms. Hope and I told the sorors to go into the opposite locker room and get prepared. Each of them had a set of skates, a helmet, and a hockey jersey with their APF name on the back hanging up in individual lockers.

We told the men to come out onto the ice first. They had on skates, helmets and black, lace-up jock straps with "APF" embroidered on the seam. They each had to take a place beside one of the swings. Then the sorors came out wearing nothing but the jerseys, helmets and skates. They all took a place next to the man of their choice, leaving two fine specimens for my sister and me. Once everyone was on the ice, we handed out hockey sticks so the games could begin.

For the next thirty minutes, everyone worked up a sweat as we dashed in and out from between the swings, playing hockey—the men against the women. There were no goalies but we roughed them up pretty bad. I was pushing my dude into the sides of the rink with my stick and then yanking on his balls through his jock strap. He had a combination painful/delighted look on his face. He was about five-ten, dark-skinned and I could tell that he hit the gym daily. He was not Kevin though.

I will not lie. I was beginning to struggle with the thought of doing the APF thing and the relationship thing with Kevin. He was falling hard and fast and so was I, in many ways. But I had to block that out of my head for the moment. Hope and I were hosting this particular freak night and we would not be out-shined by any of the others.

After everyone had worked up a sweat, we dimmed the lights

and started slow-dragging on skates to all the old fuck jams like "Do Me Baby" by Prince, "Whip Appeal" by Babyface, and "Endless Love" by Diana Ross and Lionel Richie. The jerseys and jock straps came off sometime during the process and then it was a complete free-for-all.

I got into the sex swing and my freak of the week could not wait to slide his dick up in me. I told him, "Hold up! No glove, no love!"

He sighed and put on a Headstrong and then glared at me.

I spread my legs like an eagle's wings in the swing and started fingering my pussy with my right hand. "Oh, do I sense some animosity?" I took my fingers out and licked them. "We don't have to do this, you know? I am sure one of the other men in here will be glad to hook a sister up."

"Naw, hell naw," he replied, looking sexy and mad at the same time. "Nobody's hooking your fine ass up but me."

"Then get to hooking." I pulled him closer to me on his skates and started caressing his condom-clad dick. "Damn, baby, what do they put in the water in your neighborhood? I haven't seen a big, juicy dick like this in a minute."

That got him to blush. "Oh, yeah? Well, wait until you see what I can do with it. You want the slow stroke or the punisher?"

"Um, punish me. I don't want any doll-baby shit. I want you to sweat all these curls out my damn head."

"Oh, I'm going to give you the workout of a lifetime."

I smirked. "But don't touch me."

He was taken aback. "What?"

"Don't actually touch me." I laughed. "That's one of the best things about a sex swing. Two people can fuck the hell out of one another without ever actually touching."

His curiosity was obvious. "How so?"

"Hold on to the sides of the swing stand and I'll spread my legs and move toward you. Then you have to maneuver your dick in me without touching me. Cool?"

"Hey, as long as you're giving up some pussy, I'm willing to take it any way I can get it."

I was instantly turned off and really wanted to see Kevin. I wondered what he was doing, at that very moment. Reading a book on Ancient Egypt or going over some accounting papers for the university. Possibly watching *CSI: Miami* or catching a game.

Normally during freak nights my mind was totally all about the activities. Not that night. I felt a twinge of guilt as the other dude entered me on that swing. He was an all right lover but I yearned to push him away from me. I had to save face though. Hope and the other sorors would have been pissed, if I showed out and threw a monkey wrench in the entire game plan.

We all fucked in the swings for the next hour or so and then Hope and I went into the back and came out with the "dessert" of the evening: dildos made out of ice. She and I had made them the night before, after reading the instructions on the Internet. You can find any kind of shit on the Internet, from how to make ice dildos to how to construct a bomb.

All the men were told to fuck us with the dildos and I have to admit, having that big chunk of ice inside my pussy, hitting my G-spot—we made them curved—drove me insane. That was the most incredible feeling and I came like a geyser.

As everyone was leaving and we stayed behind to clean up, I was glad that the night was over. I damn sure would be making some more ice dildos.

"What's wrong with you?" Hope asked me as we finished breaking down the swing sets.

"Nothing. Why do you ask?"

"Because I can tell something's wrong with you. I am your twin, remember?"

"I'm tired; that's all," I stated reassuringly. "We have a long drive tomorrow and we still have to take all this shit to the APF prop storage."

The sorors maintained a storage space at a local facility. We had all kinds of freaky shit in there, to be used during various freak nights. We all put in money during the investment club meetings held monthly—on nights other than during our fuck sessions—for the "gadgets."

"We'll be done in a flash, if you hurry your ass up."

I threw one of the dildos at her that was tossed on the ice.

"Don't throw that shit at me, Faith. You don't know whose pussy that was in."

"What does it matter?"

"That's plain nasty. Ewww."

"Oh, please, Hope. Now you have morals?"

Hope frowned and threw the dildo back at me. I ducked right on time and it fell on the ice and slid across the vast rink.

"We should leave that shit here," I joked. "I can see one of the mothers bringing their toddler to lessons tomorrow and finding it."

Hope laughed. "It's a pleasant visual but we can't do that. Poor kid might be traumatized for life."

"Remember when Momma used to take us to Allen's Pond for lessons in the winter?" I asked.

"I remember you falling on your ass every five seconds."

"Whatever, label whore!"

"I bet that I can beat you in a race up in this bitch. Tired or not."

I decided to take Hope up on her challenge. "You're on. Five times back and forth. Loser has to drive to the storage space and then back to the dorm."

"Oh, well, shit. I'm going to win."

Before I could get in position to say, "Ready, set, go," Hope had already taken off.

"Wait, hooker!" I yelled after her as I chased her.

We had a ball, acting like little girls again that night. Fucking and then ice skating; what a combination.

HOPE

We got to Atlanta around dinnertime the next day. Faith drove most of the way to Atlanta. I was still tired from the night before. I won the race, probably because I cheated and took off before she was ready, but it was what it was.

We snuck in quietly through the front door of our parents' house. Momma was in the kitchen, cooking up a storm. I could make out the scent of her fried chicken right away. And the smell of her mouth-watering chocolate cake. Two of my favorites.

"You're still too sexy for your shirt," Faith blurted out once we had a visual on her.

Momma had on a red blouse and some jeans. She can fill out a pair of jeans like a twenty-year-old. Her body shows no sign—to this day—of pushing out a set of big-headed twins decades earlier.

Momma spun around and threw her hand over her mouth.

"Dang, Momma," I said. "You remembered we were coming, didn't you?"

She came closer and hugged me. "Of course, why do you think I'm making your favorites, Hope." She turned to Faith and hugged her next. "Look at my babies. You've grown."

Faith giggled. "Momma, we've only been away at school for a few months and our growing years are over."

"She says that every time we go to D.C. and come back," I reminded Faith. "Where's Daddy?"

"He ran to the store to get ice cream for the cake," Momma answered. "Dinner will be ready in about twenty minutes. You need help with your luggage?"

Faith nodded toward me. "Somebody had to pack several bags to come home for the weekend."

Momma laughed. "Some things never change."

"Ha, ha, ha," I said with disdain. "I'm not that bad. For your information, Faith, I brought *some* of my clothes with me so I could leave them here and get other ones. Our closets in the dorm are not but so big and the weather will be changing soon."

"Excuses. Excuses." Faith went over to the stove and took the lid off a pot. "Ooooo, sweet potatoes. You put it down, Momma."

"It's not every day I get to cook for my two favorite daughters."

"We're your only daughters." I opened the fridge. "Did you get that fruit punch I like from the Dutch market?"

"Yes, and the maple turkey bacon for breakfast." Momma sighed. "I know about your hearty appetites. You both got that from your father."

Faith put her arm around Momma's shoulders. "And we got our stunning looks from you."

We all laughed as we sat down at the table to catch up.

★★★

Daddy and I were playing Scrabble in his study after dinner while Momma and Faith were in the family room watching *Law and Order: Special Victims Unit*. Both of them are addicted to that series.

"So, how's school?" Daddy asked me.

"Everything's fine, Daddy." I made the word "PROTECT" and Daddy frowned, letting me know that he did not have anything to cross it with. "I can't wait until graduation."

"I'm so proud of you. Both of you." He exchanged three of his tiles and it was my turn again. "Since you made the word 'PROTECT,' I guess this is a good time to ask about…"

"Daddy, Faith and I both are using protection. It's not even like that. You act like we're whores or something."

Daddy glared at me. "I never said that, but you're grown women and grown women do grown things. I'm nobody's fool, Hope."

"You're right, Daddy. It just seems so sixties. Talking to your father about sex. Who does that these days?"

"I'm not the typical father. At least, I hope not. I want to make sure that you and your sister don't get bogged down with kids before you're ready."

"Well, you don't have to worry about that. I'm not even seeing anybody… not really."

"What about Faith?"

I sighed and used the "R" in "PROTECT" to make the word "RAZOR," getting triple points for the "Z." I was kicking Daddy's ass.

"What about Faith?" I responded as I got four new tiles to put on my letter stand.

"Does she have a steady man in her life?"

"Daddy, you need to ask Faith. She's been kind of secretive with me lately."

I had an instant pain in my stomach from the guilt that kicked in. Fucking Kevin not once, but twice, had been a huge mistake. One that I was not going to repeat; no matter what.

"Secretive in what way?"

"Nothing. That came out wrong. Since it's our senior year, we've both been busy doing our own thing. We room together but a lot of times, we barely see each other in passing. She may have someone. I don't know."

"I see."

I cannot stand it when Daddy says, "I see." That means that he is either over thinking something, analyzing our every move, or imagining the worst.

"I win," I said as I used the last of my tiles to make the word "CHARGES."

"I want a rematch." Daddy chuckled. "That was a warm-up game. It's been a while since I've played you."

"That's funny because it's been the same exact amount of time since I've played you."

He reached across his desk and swatted me playfully on my head. "Cheater."

"How can a person cheat with Scrabble?"

"Where there's a will, there's a way, and I know you."

"Daddy, you lost. Suck it up like a man."

"Suck it up like a man?" He got up from his desk and walked around it. I braced myself for what was inevitably coming next: tickling. "I'll bet you won't be saying that in a second."

He started tickling me under my armpits and I could not control my laughter. Next thing you know we were rolling around on the floor, with me in tears and him enjoying making a fool out of me.

FAITH

I should have seen the ambush coming. Daddy asked me to ride with him to pick up some tools because he was building a gazebo in the backyard. Hope was always the one who would go on errands with him but she conveniently overslept that morning.

"I can't believe it's Thanksgiving already," I said from the passenger seat as we turned into the Home Depot parking lot. "Christmas will be here before we know it."

"Are you coming back home for Christmas?" Daddy parked the car, cut the ignition, and gazed at me.

"Why wouldn't we?"

"I figured Hope might come back but I wasn't sure about you."

I smirked. "Why not?"

"Hope mentioned that you have someone special in your life."

"She did?" Daddy chuckled. That's when I knew he was fabricating the truth. "No, she didn't."

"Okay, maybe she didn't go that far but she said that you've been preoccupied lately."

"I have been preoccupied, trying to get that diploma, and checking out job possibilities."

One of his eyebrows arched. "In the D.C. area?"

"In the United States of America area." I grinned. "I am seeing someone, but it's casual."

"The expression on your face is not saying casual. It's saying serious."

I reached for the latch to open up my car door. "Are we going inside or did we come here to watch people walk in and out of the store?"

Daddy opened his door and climbed out. We went in the store and were walking down the aisle with nails when he started in on me again.

"So, what's his name?"

"Kevin," I said without hesitation. "His name is Kevin."

"Student at Crockett University?"

"No, not a student. He's older than me."

"Not my age, I hope."

"No, Daddy. You're ancient."

We both laughed. In actuality, Kevin was extremely close to Daddy's age. There was no way that I was going to reveal that; not with the way he had posed his statement, with disdain in his voice.

"I know what I'm doing. Trust me. Let me make my own choices."

"Never have I tried to make choices for you. Not me or your mother. But we're always going to be concerned about you. Is that a crime?"

He picked up a pack of 40d nails and threw them into the shopping hand basket he was carrying.

"Well, is it a crime?"

"No, don't be silly. I'm glad you're concerned but, in this case, there's nothing to worry about. I'm not going to run off and elope, or let the condom break, or anything like that."

"Glad to hear you're using condoms."

"Can we drop this?"

"Sure."

When we got in line at the register, Daddy must have forgotten that we were dropping the subject.

"Has this Kevin ever been married?"

"Yes, and he's divorced."

"Kids?"

"Two gro...two sons." I caught myself before I let it slip that both Kevin's sons were grown.

"Good job?"

"Great career!" I did not have any intention of telling my father that I was dating an employee at the university. He was a worry wart and would have made up all kinds of crazy scenarios, culminating with me being ousted from school for fornicating. "I like him…a lot…and we're simply seeing what happens. Taking things day by day."

That was not exactly the truth. Kevin wanted way more than I did, but my emotions were getting caught up and I was beginning to imagine what it would be like to settle down with him.

"All that I ask is that you and your sister never allow men to disrespect you. I see all these young, desperate women—especially here in Atlanta. They settle for fragments of men instead of waiting on the total package. Real men treat women right."

"I couldn't agree with you more, Daddy."

That was the end of it. He left that topic alone and I was relieved. Once we got back to my parents' house, I was on a mission: to find Hope's ass.

She was in the attic, going through some boxes of clothes. *Did she ever stop with the clothes madness!*

"Did you save me any turkey bacon?" I asked as I approached her in the attic.

"Not any cooked bacon but there's plenty more in the fridge."

"That's jacked up. Greedy ass."

"Hey, Momma could have cooked more but she was being skimpy with the grub." Hope laughed. "Did you and Daddy find everything he needed for the gazebo?"

"Yeah, I guess. He was too busy grilling me about my dating habits."

Hope put down the black sweater she was holding and turned toward me. "Aw, I can tell by the look on your face that somehow, you're going to put a spin on this and make it my fault."

"He didn't pull the idea that I had a man out of the clear blue. You said something to him."

"I didn't say a damn thing but now that you brought it up, who are you fucking back in D.C.?"

"No one you know."

"I might shock you. I know a lot of people."

"You don't know him." For a second, I wondered if Hope might know Kevin. After all he was the CFO of our school. There was no reason for her to ever cross paths with him though. Then again, I had. "He's simply someone I met and we're kicking it."

"Humph, okay. Whatever."

My cell phone rang; it was Kevin. I answered. "Hello."

"Hey, baby," he said, sounding as sexy as ever. "Did you get to Atlanta safely? I waited for you to call me last night."

"I'm sorry. We got here and my parents were so excited to see us. We were lost in the moment, I suppose."

"Well, don't forget about me while you're down there. I miss you already."

I turned my back to Hope, as if that would prevent her from hearing what I was saying in an attic where you could hear a mouse pissing on a cotton ball. "I miss you as well. Sorry that I couldn't see you before..."

"Faith, do you know where that trunk is that has my thermal underwear in it?" Hope yelled out, interrupting me.

"Hold on." I put the phone to my chest and glared at her. "How rude! No, I don't know where the trunk is."

"Well, what good are you then?"

I rolled my eyes and went back to my conversation. "So, what are you doing for Thanksgiving?"

"Mr. Jones invited me over for dinner with his family. Since you're not here, I might as well go for it."

"That's cool. Have fun. What time are you going over there?"

"I plan to leave in a couple of hours." Kevin was silent for a few seconds and then said, "Faith, when you get back, I really want to have a serious talk with you."

"About what?"

"Matters of life."

I walked a few feet further from Hope. "Okay, we can do that. Are you sure it can wait until I get back? I can call you back in a few, but I need to go somewhere more private first."

I could hear Hope suck in air and smack her lips, but I still did not look at her.

"No, it can wait until next week. You have fun with your folks and drive safely on your way back."

"Oh, you'll be talking to me before I head back."

"No doubt. I can't go a day without my Faith fix."

"Aw, you're so sweet."

"This is sickening," Hope said to my back. "Get a room."

I waved her off in disgust. "Call me tonight, when you get back from Mr. J…" I was about to say "Mr. Jones' house" but caught myself. Hope's nosey ass would have turned into Nancy Drew in a heartbeat. "Call me later."

"Okay, baby," Kevin said. "I'll do that. Take care."

"You, too." He hung up and I turned toward Hope. "Don't even think about asking me any questions."

"I don't have any questions about your secret lover but I do want your opinion on something."

"What's that?" I asked.

Hope sat down in the window box near the front of the attic and folded her arms in front of her. "There's this girl at school and she's banging her roommate's boyfriend."

"How skank!" I spat out.

"Can I finish? Damn!" Hope frowned. "I haven't even gotten five seconds of the scenario out yet and you're already passing judgment."

"Old girl is fucking her roommate's man. What more do I need to know?"

"She didn't know he was banging her roommate at first. It was an honest mistake. She met him at a nightclub and was planning on having a one-night quickie, and he dicked her down before she even realized he knew her roommate."

"That's different. Everyone makes rash decisions when they're horny. If she really didn't know the deal, then she's in the clear. She fucked him and there was no way to take it back."

Hope stared at me. I shrugged.

"What if she fucked him again?"

"Then she's a nasty-ass ho!" I stated vehemently. "Pure and simple. Who is this skeezer? If you know her ass and she goes to Crockett, that means I must know her."

"I can't tell you. She swore me to secrecy."

I giggled. "You and I don't have secrets. It's you and me against the world. Now tell me who it is."

Hope stood up and started walking past me. "Never mind. Forget I brought it up."

"I hate it when you give up half of some juicy gossip and then don't give up the other half."

"Hey, this isn't the Young, Black and Fabulous web site."

"Whatever, tramp!"

"Come on. We need to get downstairs," Hope said. "I promised Momma that I would make the stuffing for dinner and she wants you to do the tossed salad."

"You, making stuffing? That's a scary-ass thought."

We laughed as we left out of the attic and descended the stairs, looking forward to sharing Thanksgiving dinner with our folks.

HOPE

It was clear to me that I had to give Kevin up, from head to dick. When we got back to D.C., I was prepared to avoid him at all costs. I threw myself into my studies and ignored Faith, as she sashayed in and out of our dorm room; walking on clouds. It was obvious that things were heating up between her and Kevin. She was always singing in the shower, putting on extra lotion to cover her naturally ashy knees and even whispering his name in her sleep.

Faith still refused to tell me anything about their relationship; even though I knew Kevin in the Biblical sense. I could not believe that he had never mentioned, in passing, the fucking sessions at his friend Howard's place or inside and outside of Dante's Peak. Most men like to reminisce about great sex with their women. The only conclusion that I could come to was that the two of them were breaking each other off so hard that his sex with me was not the best of the best that they had experienced. That made me feel even worse. I had fucked my sister's man and it was not even worthy of discussion. Surely if he had mentioned anything to her, she would have realized something was up.

I became depressed, knowing that Faith was getting all that good, big, juicy dick on a regular basis while I was stuck with the little boys at school. Suddenly dealing with men my own age became unappealing. I was craving something more seasoned; not decrepit but mature. A man who knew how to break a sister off right in the sex department. The ones my age were only out for self, making sure they busted nuts and not giving a damn about my needs. Except for freak nights but those only came once a month.

One day in early December, I decided to venture downtown to one of the upscale hotels. I figured that a lot of sophisticated business travelers would be hanging out in the bar. There were quite a few men in there but most were paired up having drinks and talking business. Most of them also reminded me too much of my father so they were too damn seasoned. Kevin was roughly Daddy's age but he did not look anything like him. He had a young spirit.

There was one pair of men—two African-Americans—sitting in a booth near the back. I kept my eye on them as I sat at the bar and downed a couple of Pink Ladies. My fraternal grandmother used to drink them before her death. I missed her dearly since she had passed a few years earlier after developing Parkinson's disease.

One of the men, the taller, light-skinned one, finally noticed me and smiled. I smiled back and help up my glass, like I was toasting him. He said something to his friend, who then looked in my direction. I smiled at him as well. He was extremely dark-skinned and fine as shit. Even with his tailored suit on, I could tell that he was built. They both looked to be in their late thirties or early forties. The light-skinned brother attempted to slip his wedding ring off and pass it to his friend without me noticing. When will men realize that women notice everything? Some women turn the other cheek, play dumb, and pretend like they do not know the deal; like I was about to do. I could not have cared less if he was married. His predilection for cheating was his wife's problem and not mine. I was not searching for love. I was searching for dick.

He made his way over to me and sat on the closest free stool. "Is this seat taken?"

I smirked. "It is now that you sat on it."

He grinned. "Good point. If it was taken, I would not have been able to plop down here." I took another sip of my drink, wondering if he had taken the short bus to D.C. "My name's Frank."

"I'm Effie," I told him, having already decided on my alias before I even entered the bar. I loved the role that Jennifer Hudson portrayed in *Dreamgirls* so while the name Effie normally would have made me feel a hundred-ninety years old, it felt empowering at that moment. "Effie White."

"Wow, that name sounds familiar. Do I know you from somewhere?"

I suppressed a laugh; dumb fool. "I would hope that if you knew me, you would remember me." I took my index finger and swirled it around the rim of my glass, dipped it into the cool pink liquid and then licked it. "I'm a hard woman to forget."

"You're right. I would never be able to forget you."

He sat there, staring at me, apparently struggling to find something to say. I glanced over at his friend, wondering if he was a better conversationalist.

"So, Frank, are you from D.C.?" I inquired, not really caring about all of that, but trying to get him to say something. Shit!

"No, I'm from Detroit. My friend, Andrew, and I are here on business."

"Detroit is about to be a ghost town these days, isn't it? With the automobile industry in jeopardy."

"We'll bounce back. There's no way we can let the American automobile industry fall by the wayside. Hell, we invented cars."

That was the first intelligent thing that the man had said.

"So I take it you drive an American-made car then?" I waited for him to answer but the expression on his face spoke volumes. "Oh, so you live in Detroit, probably have a lot of friends and family members who have lost jobs recently or are about to lose their jobs because of the auto industry, and you drive a foreign car?"

"My wi...I mean, a friend of mine insisted on a Lexus."

"You can say your wife." Okay, so I was not willing to play so dumb after all. I wanted him to know that his game was weak. "I saw you take your wedding ring off and hand it to your friend."

He looked nervous and flagged the bartender over. "I hope you won't hold that against me." Once the bartender was in front of him, he ordered a Heineken. "Would you like to refresh your drink?"

"Sure," I replied. "Thanks. As for holding something against you, I'm here chilling, enjoying the sights, having a few drinks. That's it. No expectations."

"Are you from D.C.?" Frank asked me.

"No, I'm from Detroit, too. In fact, the reason that I was staring at you earlier is because I know your wife." His face was about to turn blood red. "In fact, she asked me to see if I could get you to cheat on her while you were on a *supposed* business trip."

Frank struggled to catch his breath. Then, the idiot finally spoke. "But I didn't try to cheat. I never mentioned sleeping with you."

"No, not yet, but you were about to. Why else would you take off your ring?"

"I...uh...I..."

I laughed. "Take your time."

"I took it off because it was hurting my finger. I asked Andrew to hold it so that I could rest my hand."

"Do you realize how fucking dumb you sound?" I picked up my fresh Pink Lady. "You better not ever try to cheat because you cannot lie your way out of a paper bag. Faithful better be your middle name from now on."

"You're right." He jumped up from the bar. "Please don't tell Donna about this. It really was innocent."

He stumbled back to his booth, leaving his beer. He looked like someone who had seen a ghost when he relayed what had happened to his friend, Andrew. Andrew stared at me for a few seconds and then I winked. He fell out laughing when he realized that I had played his friend.

I waited a few more minutes and then walked over to their booth, delivering Frank's beer to him. As I sat down beside Andrew, who scooted over to allow it, I put the beer down in front of Frank.

"Here, you better drink this before it gets warm."

Frank glared at me, obviously because of a bruised ego. "Thanks."

"Hello, Andrew, I'm Effie White." I shook Andrew's hand, whose first name was borderline identical to my last name: Andrews. "Nice to meet you."

Andrew chuckled. "Effie White, huh? You looked different in the movie."

"Movie?" Frank inquired.

Andrew glanced at his friend and then back into my eyes. "Effie White is the role Jennifer Hudson played in the movie *Dreamgirls* and Jennifer Holliday portrayed in the stage play."

Frank looked dumbfounded. "So, you were lying to me?"

"Like you lied to me, Frankie Poo. Or at least tried to." I reached under the table and started rubbing Andrew's thigh. He did not resist, or even flinch. "Don't you think you better go call Donna and check on the kids?"

"Who said I have kids?" He looked around the bar; then at his friend. "I'm telling you, Andrew. Someone's paying her to spy on me."

Andrew sighed. "Frank, this beautiful young lady flipped the script on your macking game. She's not from Detroit because somehow, some way, I would have met her already, and she doesn't know Donna or any of your business."

"So how does she know that I have three kids?"

"Wow!" I exclaimed. "I only knew about Frank, Jr. When did you and Donna have the other two?"

"See!" Frank was about to ricochet out of the booth. "She knows about Junior."

Andrew and I fell out laughing. That was an educated guess and we both knew it. Frank was clueless.

Frank got up and straightened his suit jacket. "Andrew, we should be going. Our meeting is early tomorrow."

Andrew waved him off; especially since I was now rubbing all over his dick under the table. "I'm a night owl. You go ahead."

"Yeah, go check in with the missus," I joked. "Tell Donna that I said wassup."

Frank glared at me. "You're nothing but trouble and I cannot, and will not, leave my friend down here in this bar with you."

"Why not? You want him for yourself?" I eyed Frank up and down. "Don't tell me that you're on the downlow, too. Poor Donna. I might need to call her from my cell phone right now and tell her that she should go ahead and hire that divorce attorney that I recommended." I quickly thought of a popular street name in Detroit, a place that I had only visited once. "He has an office over on Altwater Street."

Frank's mouth fell open. I had rendered him totally speechless. He gasped for breath and then finally stomped off like a little punk.

"You're good," Andrew said, as he watched his friend panic. "Frank might have a heart attack behind that shit, *Effie*!"

"My real name's Hope," I confessed. "And your friend will be fine. I doubt he'll ever cheat on his wife again though."

"Oh, I would bet my bottom dollar on that." Andrew laughed and then placed Frank's wedding ring on the table. "He forgot to take this."

"You should tell him that you lost it. That'll teach him."

"Damn, what do you have against my boy?"

"Nothing. I don't even know him. I like fucking with people."

"I can see that."

"You like fucking with people, Andrew?" I rubbed his dick harder. It felt good under my fingertips; even through his pants. "You have a nice-size dick."

"Why, thank you. I haven't had any complaints lately."

"Lately? Oh, was it a pencil dick back in your younger years?" I grinned. "How old are you anyway, Andrew? Please tell me that you're at least thirty."

"Why? Do you have a minimum age requirement or something?"

"Kind of. I'm in my early twenties and men my age do absolutely nothing for me anymore. I need a man with vast experience."

"Well, I'm thirty-eight, Hope, and I definitely have vast experience."

"How many women have you ever fucked?"

He was taken aback, like I had asked him how many *men* he had ever fucked. "That's kind of personal, don't you think? How many brothers have you gotten down with?"

"Not nearly enough." I could tell that my response shocked him. "But I plan on adding you to my roster within the next fifteen minutes or so."

"Oh, so it's like that?"

"Yes, it is exactly like that."

"And what if I refuse?"

"You're not that crazy." I leaned over and blew in his ear. "You know you want these dick sucking lips all over your thing. Never mind about the question. I pegged you for a man whore the second I laid eyes on you."

"Man whore?"

"Yes. I'm willing to bet that you've never been married. That you don't have any kids. That you've slept with a ton of women, mostly because you have a fear of commitment. You may tend to be *boyfriendish* at times and make some women think you're digging only them, but that's merely a façade. You yank out that singles card of yours at the first sign of trouble."

Andrew shook his head. "If you think that I'm that evil, why are you sitting here rubbing on my johnson?"

"Because I came here to get fucked and you're the best candidate for the job. With man whores, I don't have to worry about anyone catching feelings or trying to be my man afterward." I released his dick and ran my fingertips down his chest. "That means we can go up to your room, presuming that you're not rooming with Frank, and do some perverted, freaky shit to each other and then move on with our separate lives."

Andrew's reply was short and to the point. "I'm not rooming with Frank."

"Then let's make moves."

★★★

F ive minutes later, we were getting off the elevator on the eighteenth floor and making our way to room 1806. I couldn't wait to get his ass inside that hotel room. Andrew was the kind of man that was made for fucking and then discarding. Any woman who would allow herself to think that he could ever exclusively belong to her was fooling herself. He was placed on the Earth to be enjoyed by the masses and to tap many asses.

When we were at the doorway and he was sticking his key card in, I informed Andrew, "I want to suck your dick first. I love sucking dick."

"You'll get zero argument from me."

"You ever had a woman put you in a suplex?"

We entered the dim room and he turned on the light switch, illuminating the posh atmosphere. There was modern leather furniture and a king-sized bed was the centerpiece of the scene. The bedding was expensive and looked extremely comfortable.

"Isn't the suplex a wrestling move?" Andrew asked.

"Exactly."

"No, I can't honestly say that I've ever wrestled with a woman."

"Well, you'll enjoy my kind of wrestling."

There was a message light on the hotel phone. "I should check that," Andrew said.

"It's probably Frank, worried about his wedding ring, or concerned that I'm in here interrogating you about his comings and goings."

Andrew laughed and took his cell phone out of his pants pocket. "Damn, I have nine missed calls from him. I forgot that I had my cell on silent."

"Told you so. Men are such creatures of nature. Your buddy wants to be a player but he's not player material."

I sat down on the bed and kicked off my shoes.

Andrew sat down beside me, lifted my left foot and started massaging it. "What makes a man player material?"

"You should know." I wiggled my toes. What he was doing felt damn good! "Here you are, with a fine, sexy stranger in your hotel room and it took you little to no effort to get me up in this camp. Just a charming smile and a banging-ass body and a few feels of your massive, elephantine dick."

"Now, I don't want you to be disappointed. I'm not working with the shortest straw in the box, but there's nothing on me resembling an elephant."

"Andrew, I already peeped out the size of your dick downstairs, remember?" I grabbed his dick again through his pants; it was hard enough to split bricks. "I like what you're working with." I pushed him down on the bed and started unbuckling his belt. He was submissive like a new puppy; a pit. "To answer your question, a player is someone who has it going on so hard that all his women can know about each other and still want to fuck him. Your boy, Frank, doesn't have it like that. Otherwise, he wouldn't give a shit if I knew his wife, Donna, or not. You feeling me?"

"That's a deep philosophy." Andrew lifted his hips slightly so I could pull his pants down around his ankles. "So you think that I'm player material?"

"I think you don't give a fuck what I think. You simply want to commence to fucking my brains out."

He chuckled because he knew my ass was on point.

"You see, I look at life differently than a lot of women. I don't believe in fantasy and I'm not delusional. Maybe back in the olden days, men might have respected women, remained faithful, and practiced reciprocity in relationships, but those days are over. Shit, women are the new men, if you really want to know the truth."

Andrew sat up on his elbows as I was undoing the laces on his expensive black leather shoes. "What the hell do you mean by that?"

"Brothers are sitting on their asses, burning out PlayStation controllers while sisters are busting their asses and paying all the bills. I'm not *that* chick, though. Women are demanding to get their pussies sucked, even though a lot of bastards still pretend like they don't get down like that. Ain't no man getting this pussy without eating it." I glared at him. "Just so you know."

He laughed. "I hear you. I love eating pussy."

"That's a good thing." I pulled his boxers down below his balls and his dick sprouted out like a tree. "Women are the only ones that get down with a real threesome. Men don't comprehend the shit." I started rubbing my hand up and down his hard shaft. "When there are two women and a man involved in a three-some, the two women understand that they're supposed to go at each other. Suck each other's tits; eat each other out; the whole damn experience."

"Threesomes are the shit!" Andrew exclaimed. "And so is your hand job."

"Humph! But let's flip the script. If I had suggested a three-some with you and Frank while we were down in the bar, you two would have come up here and tried to gang bang me instead of having an actual threesome."

"Meaning?"

"Meaning that a threesome, by definition, involves all three people fucking each other. You and your boy would have had to suck each other off and ram dicks up each other's asses for it to be a true threesome…and let me watch you go at it."

Andrew had an expression of pure disgust on his face. "Hell to the fucking no! I ain't nobody's faggot."

"If you fuck a man during a threesome, it is a sexual experience and doesn't mean you're gay, any more than a woman could be considered a lesbian if she does shit with another chick during a threesome. It's simply something to do."

Andrew frowned. "You're going make me lose my erection, if you keep talking like that."

"Shit, I don't want that to happen so I'll stop spitting the truth. You can't handle it anyway. Let's see if you can handle my suplex."

I pulled him off the bed and led him over to the sofa in the room, then pushed the coffee table out of the way.

"Damn, you're not serious about wrestling, are you?" he asked in a panic.

"No, I'm not going to slam you down or anything. Just show you a couple of my moves." I sat down on the sofa and pulled him toward me, until his dick was about to slap me in the forehead. "Come here, Mr. Detroit."

He did not hesitate to bring it and I started sucking his dick with a fury; deep throating him from the first second. I gave him a few minutes of my head action, to get him comfortable. He was moaning like a bitch, too. Then I decided to hit him with some shit that I knew he had never experienced before. I pulled his knees onto the sofa beside my hips and then slammed his chest down backward on the floor so that his dick was elevated and his head was on the carpet. He winced at first but then I bent over and started sucking him for dear life. The mixture of pain and pleasure drove him insane. It was like working out on a Nautilus machine and having your dick sucked at the same time.

Andrew started getting into it. Then he started running his fingers through my hair and whispering things like "Oh, shit!" and "Damn, baby!"

I finished him off and he exploded. I did not let him cum in my mouth. When I realized the moment was fast-approaching, I brought him to his climax with my hand and his semen spurted down and onto his chest.

After that, I rode Andrew's face for a good thirty minutes and then I slayed his dick up in that hotel room. I worked that Negro over with a vengeance and then blew him a kiss on my way out of the room.

"Leave me your number," Andrew beckoned as I was about to shut the door.

I paused and stared at him. "Thanks for the fuck, but no thanks about repeating it. It was a one-time thing. Go back to Detroit and do you." I giggled. "Tell Frank to give Donna and Frank, Jr. a kiss for me."

With that, I left out and allowed the hotel door to slam shut behind me.

FAITH

Kevin had been acting kind of strange lately. Nothing that I could put my finger on but he did not seem like himself; the man that I fell in love with. *Damn, did I say that?* Yes, I did. It was love. At least love as I knew it. I was feeling him like no other, and it was not all about the sex. It was all about him. His maturity—both mentally and spiritually. His pillow talk. His intellect. His compassion. His concern for me.

We were at this holiday bazaar in Largo, MD. The vendors had wonderful gift items for Christmas and Kwanzaa. I found this beautiful black doll for Hope, dressed in red, green and white. Even though we were way too old to play with dolls, Hope liked to collect them and there was zero doubt that she would cherish it.

I bought my mother some African jewelry for a Christmas present and I purchased a wooden African mask for Daddy.

"You're acting like Santa Claus," Kevin said, as I finished up my transaction with the vendor selling the masks.

"Christmas is a couple of weeks away. I'm not into last-minute shopping. Too stressful."

I tried to take his hand so we could walk to the next vendor, but he pulled his hand away from me and put it in his pocket.

"Faith, I wish you'd reconsider and stay here for Christmas… with me."

I felt terrible because I could tell that he was serious about wanting to share the holiday with me.

"I can't, Kevin. Hope can't drive to Atlanta alone. Neither she nor my parents would ever forgive me."

"Why can't she fly? I'll pay for her ticket," he offered.

I shook my head. "You don't know my sister." I paused in front of a female vendor who was selling body oils. I was out of my favorite—360 Degrees—and wondered if she had any. That would save me a trip to where I normally purchased it. "I really want you and Hope to meet soon."

"I'm surprised." Kevin glared at me. "It's been your practice, these past several months, to keep our relationship hidden."

"That's not true!"

"It isn't? So your parents and sister know all about me?"

I hesitated before responding, realizing that I needed to choose my words carefully.

"Well, do they know about me or not?" he asked persistently.

"They all know that I'm seeing someone *special* but they don't know any of the details."

"Can I help you with something?" the young woman behind the six-foot table asked.

"Do you have 360 Degrees?"

"Yes, what size did you want?"

"I'll take a two-ounce bottle."

"Got you covered," she said and then went about her business of squirting some from a large plastic bottle into a glass one with a roller on top.

Kevin was quiet the entire time that I finished the purchase. In fact, he walked off and deserted me. Moments later, I found him in the area where all the food vendors were located. He was grubbing down on a fried fish sandwich and drinking home-made lemonade. I was offended that he had not purchased me anything but I decided to let it go.

I sat down beside him on the bench of the table. "We should really talk about this."

He shrugged. "There's nothing to talk about. I should have known this would happen; getting involved with a little girl."

"I'm not a little girl, Kevin, and I resent that. I'm over twenty-one and I'm graduating from college next semester. Why are you talking down to me like that?"

"Because, *Faith*, you're playing games with me and only children play games. Adults do things the right way."

"If you want to end your relationship with me, all this isn't necessary. You don't have to be mean. Just tell me it's over. I can handle it."

Kevin took a sip of his lemonade through a straw and stared at me. "You don't get it, at all. I don't want to end our relationship. I want to get married."

"Married?" I asked, astonished.

"You act like it's a dirty word. Yes, married. I'm not a spring chicken like you, Faith. My window of opportunity to have the things a man craves in life is closing quickly. Either you want to build a life with me or you don't."

"Kevin, we haven't been seeing each other that long. Granted, we've moved pretty fast but...when are you talking about? Immediately?"

"I want an immediate commitment but the wedding can wait six months or so."

Six months! He was tripping!

"Kevin, I do love you. I won't lie about that."

"But? I know there's a but."

"But we need to spend a little more time getting acclimated to each other's lives before making such a hasty decision. I'm not trying to be a statistic; married and divorced once or twice before I turn thirty. Bringing kids into the world and then not raising them as a nuclear family. I only want to get married once and..."

"Let me finish the sentence for you. And you're not sure if I'm the one."

I reached over and touched his hand. "I need some time. Just a little more time. When I graduate, I'm not even sure that I'll be able to find a decent chemical engineering job in this area. All of that remains to be seen and I'm sure you're not trying to relocate. You only started working at Crockett University this year."

He pushed my hand away. "You don't have to sit here and make up excuses not to be with me, Faith. You wanted me to break up with you a few minutes ago because you're the one who wants out." He stood up and grabbed his trash off the table. "Don't let me stop you."

He walked away with much attitude, tossing his trash in a can and leaving the building. I could not believe that he was going to leave me stranded so far away from school. I jumped up and rushed outside. Seconds later, he pulled up to the curb in front of the building with a jerk, leaned over and pushed the passenger door open.

"Get in," he demanded.

I climbed in, after tossing my bags in the backseat, and he pulled off, blasting the radio the entire way back to his place.

Kevin did not speak to me for most of the night but way over in the morning, he came to me in his bed—nude—and made the most passionate love to me ever. I was confused, so confused. I did not want to lose him but I also did not want to feel pressured into marriage when I was not ready. Everything had happened so fast. One thing he was right about was that I needed to stop acting like our relationship was taboo and come clean with my family. But telling them meant hearing their opinions and listening to them pass judgment. I was not prepared to endure it, but if it would make him happy, and extinguish some of his doubt, it made sense to do it. I planned to introduce him to Hope before we left for Atlanta for Christmas.

HOPE

I was never going to fuck him again! I was never going to fuck him again! I was never going to fuck him again!

The words resonated over and over in my head, as I lay in Kevin's bed, with his head buried between my thighs. I did not mean to end up there. It was all a huge misunderstanding. Earlier that day, I was standing in the cafeteria line in the student union, minding my business and waiting for the work study coed behind the counter to put gravy over my Salisbury steak and mashed potatoes. I was trying to decide between the strawberry cheesecake and apple cobbler a little further down the food station when Kevin came up behind me and put his hands around my waist.

He whispered in my ear, "Meet me in the parking garage below the building when you finish eating."

As quickly as he appeared, he was gone. For a tall and big-ass man, he certainly had this stealth mode about him.

I went and joined my two girlfriends, who had walked over to the union with me. I listened to them go on and on about this dude and that dude while we ate. Stacy had this habit of talking with her mouth open that was straight up unappealing and enough to make someone lose their appetite. I avoided looking at her the entire time so my stomach would not churn.

"You want to go see that new Amin Joseph film, Hope? We're going to Union Station to check it out," Lindsay asked.

"No, I'm good," I replied. "I need to take care of something before the night's out. I'm writing a mock interview with Denzel Washington for Ms. Heller's class."

"Damn, too bad you can't interview Denzel for real," Stacy said. "You ever get that shot, let me know. I don't care if you're about to sit his ass down in a hotel in Dubai for a chat, I'll be on the first plane smoking out this bitch!"

Lindsay rolled her eyes. "She said a mock interview and you're getting all hot and bothered. Calm down. If you ever saw that man for real, you'd probably faint."

Stacy smirked. "I would faint right into his damn arms. I love me some older men. There's something about them."

I glared at her. "Is that why you've been talking about all the boys you've been banging from school this whole time?"

Stacy nudged Lindsay. "I know she's not talking to me, like she hasn't bedded half the football team over the past four years."

Lindsay laughed and jerked her head to the left, toward the entrance where Raheem was walking in with some of his teammates. "Speaking of which."

I stood up and grabbed my tray. "Fuck both you hookers."

They giggled and slapped each other a high-five as I stomped off. Raheem tried to grab my elbow and stop me but I kept it moving. When I got out into the lobby, I had two choices. I could walk out the front door or walk over to the elevator and press the down button for the garage. I chose the latter.

Kevin was waiting in his Mercedes and I climbed in. Before I could utter a word, his hand was up my skirt and pushing my already soaked panties to the side. I did not resist; I spread my legs wider. I needed some release.

He pulled his hand out and licked his fingers. Then, he said, "I can't wait to get you home."

★★★

Less than an hour later, there I was, letting Kevin eat my pussy and feeling guilty and exhilarated at the same time. I was in a daze. I had my arms spread out at my sides, figuring that if I did not touch him and only let him do his damn thing on me, that it would cut down on my responsibility as far as doing Faith wrong.

Kevin was going to town on my pussy that day, more so than ever before. It was like he was attempting to suck my life force right out of me. I came with a vengeance and smothered his face. He moaned and said, "Um, yummy," and went right back at it.

I lifted my hips and started grinding my pussy on his tongue, which he was darting in and out of me like he was doing pushups with it. I closed my eyes and got into it even more and was about to climax again until...

Kevin whispered, "You taste so good, Hope."

I was frozen in time, with my hips elevated in the air, my eyes widened in shock, and my mouth flung open. I pushed him off me and leapt from the bed.

"What the fuck did you say to me?"

He turned over on his back on the bed and stared up at the ceiling, not uttering a word.

"Did you say what I thought you said?" I asked, already knowing the answer.

"It was bound to happen," he replied. "Sooner or later, I had to fuck it all up."

I backed up to the window of his bedroom on weak knees. Then I grabbed my shirt and pulled it over my head, not bothering to put my bra back on.

"You fucking bastard!"

"Oh, now, Hope, don't play innocent with me." Kevin chuckled and sat up, staring at me. "It's not like you didn't know you were fucking Faith's man this entire time."

I was now pulling on my panties with one hand and groping for my skirt with the other.

"How could you do this to my sister?"

He winked and grinned. "How could you?"

"So, you've known all along. You sick fuck."

"Hey, that night at Dante's Peak, I gave you a hint. I told you that I missed you before I kissed you. You went for it anyway."

I thought back to that night and he was right. Drunk as I was, I remembered him saying that he missed me—more than once—like a long-lost lover.

"I wasn't thinking clearly that night. I was drunk."

"You weren't too drunk to feed me some pussy in the booth and then fuck me in my car."

"How did you know?"

"I knew that Faith wasn't out clubbing that night. I spoke to her less than five minutes before I walked in Dante's Peak. When I spotted you, I realized you were her twin. Every man has a fantasy about fucking twins, if only for once in their lifetime. I saw an opportunity and I made my move...and I got what I wanted."

"I didn't know you were dating my sister. This is all your fault," I lashed out at him.

"Not at first but you knew before the night was over. I said her name in the car on purpose, to see where your head was. To see if you would stop me. You didn't. You kept your legs spread and let me keep feeding dick to your pussy."

Kevin walked off into the hallway and then into the kitchen. I followed him, fully dressed except for the shoes I was carrying by the straps in my left hand.

He went into the fridge and drank some fruit punch straight out the plastic jug, and then belched. All the class that I thought he possessed, that I had risked my relationship with my twin sister over, suddenly disappeared. He was the biggest piece of shit of all.

"When I saw you walking along the street that day, right before Thanksgiving, I decided to go for it again. Why the hell not!"

"Why the hell not?" I stated sarcastically. "Because it was the wrong fucking thing to do."

Kevin shrugged. "Again, you did it. I didn't force you over my boy's place. I didn't force you to do a damn thing and I didn't force you to come over here today."

"Faith adores you; that's obvious from all the time she's been spending with you."

"Does she talk about me to you?"

I could see anguish mixed up in that question.

"Does she ever mention me to you, Hope? Or does she allow me to remain some nameless, faceless lover that she's ashamed of?"

As realization dawned on me, I sat down on the corner of his kitchen table. "Aw, now I get it. You're fucking me to punish my sister. Because she won't openly declare some undying love and admiration for you, you're paying her back by messing around with me. I'm nothing but a pawn in your sick-ass game."

Kevin did not respond. He turned his back to me and pretended to be cleaning out his sink.

"Don't get all silent on me now," I said, going over to him and forcing him to turn around and look down at me. "You're wounded and now you're on the attack."

"Men have feelings, too. Women fail to realize that."

"So you think it's okay to wound others because you're wounded."

Kevin suddenly started chuckling. "Listen to you, with all your self-righteousness. You've been doling out pussy to me out both sides of your drawers and now you want to chastise me. If you're so honest and forthright, then go tell Faith the truth. Tell her what you've been up to."

"I...I..."

"Cat got your tongue, Hope?" He laughed again. "Go tell Faith that I've been using you. That I've been fucking you behind her back and pretending like I didn't know it was you laying it on a brother. Explain how it all happened. Not once, not twice, but three times."

"I hate your fucking guts!"

"You might hate me but I bet, if I was willing and you had the chance, you would fuck me again." He started rubbing my breasts through my clothing with both hands. "Come on. Let's go back in my bedroom and finish our business. Then I'll drop you off at school."

Damn shame that I had a moment of weakness and actually contemplated his proposition for a few seconds. Then common sense kicked in.

"Get the fuck off of me!" I pushed him away and headed for his front door, in bare feet and still holding my shoes by the straps.

"Okay, okay," he said, walking behind me. "At least let me drive you home. That way, we can talk."

I swung around to face him. "Talk about what?"

"Our plans for next semester. I was thinking about going away for the weekend...maybe to the Poconos. I can rent a log cabin and we can fuck by the fire and out in the snow."

"You are really crazy!"

I opened the door and he attempted to hold me back by the elbow. "Let's go back in my room."

I managed to free myself and rush out the door. As I put my shoes on out front and then hailed down a taxi to take me back to school, I was totally distraught. What the hell was I going to do?

FAITH

I had been waiting in Kevin's office for about ten minutes before he entered, after finishing up a meeting.

"Hey, there," he said, obviously surprised to see me sitting at his desk.

I got up, put my arms around him and kissed him as he leaned down to reciprocate.

"Hey, baby. I hope you don't mind me stopping by."

He shut the door to the outer office. "Not at all."

"Your secretary must have stepped away."

"She's out sick today. The flu."

"Wow, I hope she feels better."

"She'll be fine. It's going around. It's that time of year. I really need to get a flu shot."

I grimaced. "Good luck with that. The last time that I got a flu shot, I was sick for three weeks."

"Then maybe I won't get a flu shot."

We both laughed as we got settled on the couch in his office.

"So what brings you here?" Kevin asked.

"I missed you. My sister and I are headed home in the morning and I didn't want to leave for winter break without saying good-bye."

"You could always change your mind and stay here. My offer for a plane ticket for your sister still stands."

I caressed his hand. "That's sweet but it won't fly. She'll never agree to it." I crossed my legs and scooted closer to him. "But I have decided to come back early. We're going to drive back early on New Year's Eve. That way you and I can bring in 2009 together."

He grinned from ear to ear. "That sounds great. By the way,

I got us some tickets to one of the inauguration balls; the one being held by the HBCUs at the Postal Museum."

"Oooh, that's wonderful. I still can't believe we have an African-American president."

"I believe it. It was for him and it is our time."

"It is our time, Kevin." I gazed into his eyes lovingly. "I've been thinking long and hard about what you said…about getting married and settling down."

"And?"

"And you're right. I need to be more considerate of your needs and stop being so selfish. You're older and you want things out of life. You shouldn't have to place your life on hold for me."

Kevin sat up on the edge of the sofa. "Faith, are you being sincere? Don't joke with my feelings."

"I would never take your feelings for granted. I love you, Kevin."

"You'll marry me?"

"Yes." I stood up and walked over to the door. "I was thinking a June wedding. I realize it seems cliché but it has always been my favorite month. A numerologist told me once that June was my lucky month."

"And what is your unlucky month?" he asked.

"December." I locked the door. "This month."

"Well, obviously that numerologist wasn't all that. If this is your unlucky month, you wouldn't be getting engaged."

"True that." I started taking off my blouse.

"What are you doing?"

"Consummating our commitment to each other."

"We can't have sex here; in my office," Kevin protested.

"We have before. At least, oral sex, but sex is sex." I walked toward him, removing my underwear along the way. "I want you."

"We can go back to my place. I can leave right now. My meetings are done for the day."

I pushed him down on the couch and then straddled him. "I can't wait that long."

He returned my kisses with passion and then it was on. I ended up bent over the couch, on my knees, with him fucking me roughly from behind.

"That's right," I said, "Show me how much you really want me, Kevin."

He fucked me so hard that my head was banging up against the pillows on the couch and my neck was strained. I let him keep going though. I needed him to do it that way.

He climaxed and pulled out, with the Headstrong rubber dangling and full of his semen.

Struggling for breath, he asked, "When do you want to go ring shopping?"

"As soon as I get back," I replied. "But I'll tell you this. You try to slide anything smaller than two karats on my finger and all bets are off."

He chuckled. "I wouldn't dream of it."

I started putting my clothes back on.

"Want to grab some dinner?" he asked, slapping me on the ass. "I'm starving."

"I can't. I need to get back to the dorm."

"Okay. So what time do you leave tomorrow?"

"Early. Traffic is going to be a bitch so we need to make waves and get on down the road." I paused and then glanced at him. "I have an idea. Since we're going to tie the knot, I have to bring you out of the proverbial closet. Why don't you fly down to Atlanta for a few days and get to know my family?"

Kevin seemed taken aback. "Are you for real?"

"Yes, of course. You keep wanting to purchase a plane ticket, so purchase your own. That way you can meet all the other important people in my life at the same time."

I could tell that he was someplace else; somewhere deep in thought.

"That might be a bit too much and a bit too fast," he finally blurted out.

"You're the one who wants to get married right away, and now you want to slow things down?"

"Let me think about it," he said. "Mr. Jones invited me over his house on Christmas Day and I don't want to lose my brownie points. Plus one of my sons mentioned he might fly in to spend Christmas with me."

"You don't have to come on Christmas. What about the day after? You can even buy a one-way ticket and then ride back with Hope and me on New Year's Eve."

"Like I said, let me think about it."

There was an apparent animosity in Kevin's voice.

"If you're not ready, I understand."

"No, no, I'm ready. I'll look into flights tonight. It might be tight trying to get availability, since it's the holidays."

"You're the man. I'm sure you'll find something."

"And then I have to find a hotel."

"No way. I wouldn't hear of it. My parents have a spare bed-room."

"I can't show up at your parents' house for the first time and stay there."

"You're not some random Negro off the street. We're getting married. They need to get to know you, so they can accept this. My sister, especially. She's very picky and protective when it comes to men who come around me."

"Is that right?" The sarcasm was evident. "What about her own man? Does she have one?"

"Hope believes in freedom of sexual expression. I can't fathom her settling down with a man before she's forty." Kevin grew quiet. "I'm coming down with a headache. Can you get me a bottle of water out the machine down the hall? I have some Motrin in my purse."

"Sure, baby."

Kevin left out of the office to get my bottle of water. By the time he came back from the vending machine alcove, I was gone.

★★★

Hope was waiting for me behind a huge oak tree on the opposite side of the street from the administration building.

"Did you get it?" she asked before I could open my mouth to speak.

"Yeah, I got it," I replied and then handed her a small high-definition, hard drive camcorder.

"Do you think he suspected anything?"

I shook my head. "Not a chance. He's probably in there right now searching Orbitz for cheap flights to Atlanta."

She gazed at me. "Are you upset that you had to do that?"

"No, it's cool. What had to be done had to be done. Now, let's finish this."

Hope and I walked off together toward our dorm, in silence.

HOPE

Later that evening, Faith and I were on our way out of Mr. Jones' office. As the vice president of Crockett University and a close confidante of ours during our four years there, we felt he was the best person to approach about the subject of Kevin Nelson.

Imagine his surprise—and disgust—as we relayed our story to him. We told him all about how "Mr. Nelson" had been taking advantage of both of us over the span of his first semester at the school. How after Mr. Jones had introduced Faith to him that day, he had shown up outside one of her classrooms in the engineering building less than a week later. How he had lured her into a sordid affair because we were having trouble keeping up with our tuition payments, in light of the state of the current economy. How he then insisted that I begin sleeping with him as well since he had always had this fantasy about bedding twins. How he had even had sex with both of us in his office on various occasions, as evidenced by the videotape evidence we presented him.

There was no audio on the tape. We made sure of that. We also made sure that nothing on the tape would make anyone speculate that Faith had been the aggressor of the sexual act. All Mr. Jones saw was Faith bent over the couch, being fucked mercilessly from behind from the angle of the camcorder that had been hidden on Kevin's bookshelf among various finance books.

We told Mr. Jones that neither of us wanted to continue being forced into performing lewd sexual acts with "Mr. Nelson" and that our real concern was other young ladies that he might take advantage of sexually in the future—or possibly other current victims. Being the chief financial officer of the university gave him carte blanche access to student records and direct knowledge of who may be struggling to stay in school.

As we walked out of Mr. Jones' office, Faith and I both realized that Kevin's goose was cooked; charred even. His career at

Crockett would soon be over and he would be lucky if he ever worked in the same field again.

We decided to leave for Atlanta that night. Why wait around for the asshole to show up at our dorm to cause a scene? He was blowing up Faith's cell phone but to no avail. She was not about to answer and he never had my number.

Once we got near Richmond, about two hours out of D.C., we finally had the heart-to-heart conversation that was well overdue.

"Do you think we did the right thing?" Faith asked from the passenger seat of our Hummer H3. "We did lie to Mr. Jones. Kevin never forced either one of us into anything and it was never about money."

"Granted, we took some liberties with the truth but…"

"Some?"

"Okay, we took a lot of liberties with the truth, but he deserved all of it and then some." I honked at a slow-ass driver; probably a local who was in no hurry and was doing five below the speed limit in the left-hand lane. She moved out of my way when she noticed the size of my vehicle and headlights. "The nerve of him. A grown-ass man, old enough to be our father, playing with both of our emotions like that."

I could see the anger in Faith's eyes; even in the near darkness.

"Faith, I was wrong too. I was weak. He made me get all caught up in him and I did some really stupid and ridiculous things. I know you're mad and you should be. I would be pissed off if you did that shit to me."

She remained silent; just glaring at me.

"Look at it this way. I could have kept doing it. I could have gone away with him to the Poconos for the weekend like he wanted. I could have done a lot of dirty, skanky things but I didn't. I cut his ass off."

"You only cut him off because you found out he played you!" Faith yelled suddenly, almost causing me to swerve off the road. "This is not about your concern for me! This is about your selfishness! In all our years on this earth, we have never fucked the same man. At least, I don't think we have."

"This was the first time, I assure you," I said with disdain. "I'm not trying to get down with your leftovers."

"But that's exactly what you did. Even if I believe you about the shit that went down at Dante's Peak, what about the other times? What the hell were you thinking?"

I could have easily lashed out at Faith, talking a bunch of shit, and trying to deflect the guilt off of myself but decided that was not a smart move. Not with another eight hours or so before we reached Atlanta. Instead, I jerked the car off Interstate-95 onto an off-ramp.

"We need gas," I announced. "And I need something with some damn caffeine in it."

"Let me drive," Faith suggested. "I think better when I drive."

I pulled up to the gas pump and hopped out, stuck my credit card into the slot and then took the gas cap off the truck. Faith disappeared inside the convenience store and into the ladies room. I knew that she was in there cursing me out, probably slamming shit against the wall, and trying to regain her composure. By the time she came out of the restroom, I was in line to pay for a soda and a bag of chips.

"You want anything?" I asked as she walked past me and back outside.

When I got back to the truck, Faith was waiting on the driver's side.

"I've got this," I told her.

"I'm driving."

I tried to get around her to open the driver's door.

"I said, I'm driving," she repeated.

"Faith, stop playing and move out the way."

She pushed me...hard.

"Oh, so now you want to get rough with me?" I asked, getting pissed. "I'm not going to fight you over a man, Faith."

"This isn't about Kevin. This is about me and you."

She pushed me again...harder.

I set my soda and chips down on the hood of the truck. "Now I'm not going to take that shit a third time. I don't give a shit how mad you are ab—"

Faith hauled off and punched me in my face. I was stunned. My sister had never hit me before. A playful slap here and there; a pinch on the arm; a slight, fake kick on the ass. But she punched me...hard.

I lost it and hit her in the stomach, right in the gut.

"Oh no, the fuck you didn't!" she exclaimed and then pushed me to the ground and started wailing on me.

I tried to push her off of me but she was a madwoman. She was punching and scratching and I was yanking her hair with one hand and pulling her ear with the other. I heard someone yell, "They're out here fighting!" and then a crowd of people stood around watching us.

One of the male attendants rushed out the convenience store and tried to separate us, but once he had Faith lifted up off me, she turned around and squeezed his nuts, causing him to double over in pain.

"Stay the fuck out of this," Faith warned him—and the others.

It took the police another five or six minutes to get there. By that time, both of us had busted lips, hair that had been ripped out of our heads was scattered all over the concrete, and there was a huge dent in the Hummer from where I had braced myself while Faith was pulling me backward onto the ground to scrap.

We ended up in separate jail cells in at the Richmond County Jail on Walton Way. They were directly across from each other. We stared at each other like we wanted to murder one another. Then Faith started laughing and it became contagious.

"What are you laughing about?" I asked, trying to hold back my own chuckling.

"Look at us. In jail, over a stupid-ass motherfucker who's probably knee deep in another woman's pussy at this very moment."

I fell out laughing, envisioning it.

"Naw, he's probably hunting for our asses on campus. Mr. Jones has surely made it clear that his career is over by now and he knows about our lies."

"Fuck that six-eight piece of shit," Faith said. "He deserves everything he gets."

I stopped laughing and turned serious. "I really am sorry, Faith. I don't know how I can ever make it up to you, but whatever you want me to do, I will."

Faith's laughter subsided as well. "You didn't mean it; I realize that. I know you better than anyone else on the planet and we both have been stuck on stupid over some dick before. How do you think I feel? I was damn near ready to marry him and have his babies. How fucked up is that?"

"That would have been fucked up," I agreed.

"In a way, this Jerry Springer moment is a good thing. Not the way it all went down but I needed to find out what kind of man Kevin is. If he's capable of fucking you, he would have been cheating like crazy during our entire relationship."

"True that."

"Besides, I had no business thinking about settling down right now anyway. We're about to graduate. We have our careers ahead of us. He would've held me back and, at the end of the day, I would've wasted a lot of valuable time for nothing."

I nodded my head. "He's not worthy of you. Men are full of shit. That's why I play the field. I meet a man, use him for the only thing he's good for, and then I bounce."

"That's the APF way," Faith joked. "Damn, wait till the sorors hear about this."

"You think we should tell them?" I asked, not quite comprehending the reasoning behind the thought.

"Hell yes. We have to tell them. The sorors of Alpha Phi Fuckem Sorority, Inc. keep no secrets from each other. Didn't you read the handbook?"

"I memorized the entire handbook, hooker."

"Whatever, label whore."

I giggled. "I may be a label whore but even here, in lockdown, I look damn good."

At that, Faith and I sat there and laughed and joked and reminisced until our parents showed up the next morning to bail us out and to get the Hummer out of impound. All charges were dropped after Faith and I threw ourselves at the mercy of the female judge during our arraignment. Even as a judge, she was still a female, and understood that dick makes women do silly things.

Our parents were not quite as understanding about the events. They wanted to know if we both needed therapy. Once we were back in Atlanta, we had an old-fashioned family meeting—like some sixties shit—and decided that we had to put the past in the past. Daddy wanted to find Kevin and put a bullet right between his eyeballs but we convinced him to let it go. We assured him that nothing like that would ever happen again. No one could come between two twins.

FAITH

September 2009
Sioux Falls, South Dakota

Good thing that I did not marry Kevin's ass. It would have been a long distance marriage for sure. I ended up in Sioux Falls, South Dakota, of all godforsaken places. Other than a St. Patrick's Day parade and a jazz festival, there was not going to be much for me to look forward to. All of that aside, I had landed a great job with a chemical plant making close to six figures right out of college, so it was all good. Besides, the world is a big place and if you only see a small part of it, you are missing out.

I did not plan to be in South Dakota more than a few years. I missed my parents and of course, I missed Hope. Her lucky ass ended up landing a job with the *Los Angeles Times* as an entertainment reporter. All those mock interviews that she wrote while she was in Ms. Heller's class senior year had paid off. She had actually gotten to meet Denzel and I had to hold the phone away from my ear for the entire ten minutes that she was screaming about the experience afterward.

I was still in the process of trying to make friends and it was not an easy task. The people that I worked with were brainiacs and all of them were either married or shacking up. There were no "men of interest" at my job and besides, I had learned my lesson about shitting where I eat. I had followed that rule to the letter until I started fooling around with Kevin Nelson, and we know how that turned out.

I was going to take things slow, get to know myself, and keep a collection of about ten dildos and vibrators to get me through the dick drought. There was no APF chapter in Sioux Falls but I was hellbent on changing that. It would take time to find the right candidates. Not every woman is APF material. That's for damn sure.

I was looking forward to the Alpha Phi Fuckem Convention in Jamaica in a couple of months. The conventions are always off the fucking chain. That's when the older sorors, the ones who have been sexually liberated since before Hope and I were born, educate us pups on everything from dick sucking to investing our money wisely. More than two thousand usually show up. Damn! Dick, sun, and fun in Jamaica. Time could not waste away fast enough for me.

I went into my office, closed the door, and dialed Hope. She answered on the third ring.

"What you doing?" I asked, trying to live my life vicariously through her.

"On my way to Rodeo Drive to meet up with that new female rapper Reaction to interview her."

"Oh, I don't know her music."

"But you will. She's the next hottest thing."

"Cool. Then what are you doing?"

"Having dinner with one of the sorors from the L.A. chapter."

"I hate you," I joked.

"No one told your ass to move to South Dakota. I don't give a rat's behind how much they are paying you, the trade off is not worth it."

"So find me a job in Los Angeles and I'm on the first plane."

"Don't tempt me because I'll fuck somebody to land you a job out here, if I have to."

"No, I'm not trying to pimp you out like that."

"Just say the word."

We both laughed.

"I love you, Hope."

"I love you, Faith."

I hung up my phone and fought to hold back tears. I could do what had to be done. After all, Soror Ride 'em High is the shit.

ABOUT THE AUTHOR

Zane is the publisher of Strebor Books/ATRIA Books, a division of Simon and Schuster. She is the creator and co-executive producer of *Zane's Sex Chronicles*, a Cinemax original series. She is the *New York Times* bestselling author of more than a dozen titles and she resides in the Washington, D.C. area. You can visit her on the web at www.eroticanoir.com.

ONE TASTE

BY ALLISON HOBBS

CHAPTER 15

Matt gave a mental sigh when he spotted the short, light-skinned, barrel-shaped young woman wearing a bright red jacket, black pants, and black ankle boots waiting outside the Recovery House. On the ground beside her boots was an oversized plastic trash bag. The trash bag could only mean trouble for Matt. Apparently, the girl was leaving the House and needed a lift to her next dwelling place.

When Matt pulled his van up to the curb, the roly-poly girl picked up the trash bag and slung it over her shoulder. Approaching the van, looking like Mrs. Santa Claus, Onika's girlfriend waved excitedly. She pulled open the door, climbed inside, and threw her trash bag in the back, and squeezed into the passenger seat with Onika. "Whaddup, Onika!"

"Ain't shit'," Onika said dryly.

"Aw, don't be acting all down and out on our first night as roomies."

Matt's jaw dropped. "Onika, what's she—"

"There you go," Onika spat. "Why you gotta be all up in my business?"

"I have a right to know who—"

"Nigga, you ain't got a right to know nothing!"

Puddin laughed. "Damn, Onika, didn't your mother teach you to respect your elders?"

"Yeah, but I only give it when I get it," Onika replied sullenly. "I think it's disrespectful for a nigga to be trying to mind my business."

"You got a point," Puddin agreed.

"I've never disrespected you, Onika," Matt declared, trying to ignore the fact that Puddin had referred to him as an elder. Since when did being thirty-nine years old equate to being an elder? Matt wondered, peeved. "How have I disrespected you?" he persisted.

"Man, would you please pull off from in front this damn Recovery House," Onika spat. "Shit, I still owe room and board at that bitch."

Matt didn't move. "I asked you how I've ever disrespected you."

Onika sucked her teeth. "Aiight, sit out here if you want to, but if the house manager or somebody tries to come at me, starting some shit about the rent, you better be prepared to come out of your pocket 'cause I ain't giving up a damn thing."

Puddin fell out laughing and slapped Onika's palm. "I know that's right, girl. After they broke up the fight between me and that new chick, Miss Betina gon' tell me I had to go, then she had the nerve to start adding up how much I owed. Now, you know I told her to kiss my big ass."

Onika chuckled briefly and then shot Puddin a curious look. "So, why was you and the new chick fighting?"

Puddin dug inside her purse and opened her palm, revealing a handful of pills. "Bitch snuck some Oxycontin in the house and wasn't trying to share. Now, you know I loves me some Oxy, so I burned her for all her shit. When she tried to accuse me of taking her shit, I busted her mouth."

Smiling, Onika shook her head as if Puddin was a mischievous four year old. Matt felt a dislike for Puddin that was so intense, he wanted to pull over and physically toss the pill-popping addict out of his van. He didn't have time to compete for Onika's attention. Now that he'd heard Puddin's story, he knew the pudgy little freeloader would be hanging around forever. He wanted to kiss and make up with Onika as quickly as possible. He didn't have all night. He had a job to do, and men to supervise and transport back to their group home. But with a third wheel in his and Onika's love nest, diffusing his baby girl's anger would take a lot more time and patience than he had tonight. He could only pray that Puddin would take every one of the stolen pills as soon as they returned to the apartment. He hoped Puddin would quickly nod off into oblivion, and give him and his baby girl the privacy they deserved. Who was he kidding? It would be too much like right for Onika's ill-mannered friend to conveniently knock herself out.

Instead of parking, Matt pulled up to the door of building G and sat behind the wheel, allowing the engine to idle while Puddin got out and retrieved her trash bag. Onika sat beside him, silent. "I'm going to give you some time to cool off, baby girl. I'll give you a call after me and the boys pick up the furniture."

"Oh, it's like that, now?"

"Like what?"

"You just gon' drop me off in front of the crib like you don't give a damn how I feel?"

Matt couldn't win for losing. He was trying to give Onika the space she obviously needed and she still wasn't satisfied. Not knowing what to say, Matt held out his hands and shrugged. He caught a glimpse of Puddin standing at the door of Onika's apartment building and then he felt the buckle of Onika's pocketbook as it crashed against the side of his face.

"What the hell is wrong with you?" he shouted, rubbing his palm across his cheek.

"Why you looking out the window at Puddin? You tryin' to get with my friend?"

"Don't be ridiculous. I just glanced out the window for a moment. I wasn't paying any attention to Puddin." Matt pulled the visor down to check the damage to his face. There was some swelling and redness near his cheekbone, which meant he'd have to concoct a believable story when his wife asked what happened.

There was the sudden sound of Puddin banging on the passenger window. "I know that mufucka didn't put his hands on you!"

Onika slid down the window. "Nah, but I had to crack him upside his head—put that ass in check." She turned to Matt. "Ain't that right, baby?" she asked with a huge grin, as if being smacked with her pocketbook was something he should be proud of.

Matt looked grim. How had he allowed his world to spin so badly out of control? It was possible that Onika was crazy. But what was his excuse for going along with her nuttiness? *I'm pussy whipped*, he solemnly admitted.

"Answer me!" The humor had left Onika's voice.

Not wishing to provoke her again, Matt responded quickly. "Yeah, you keep me in check." *Ugh!* He sounded like a wimp. He rubbed the tender area on his face. The pain was tolerable. He felt more humiliated than physically hurt. He was deeply ashamed that his weakness for Onika had been witnessed by a third party.

He thought he'd made it clear that he didn't mind getting cussed out or smacked around behind closed doors. But now Onika was acting out in front of Puddin. Clearly, Onika was out of control, and Matt didn't know how to rein her back in. He yearned for the sweet, considerate young woman she'd been when he first developed an interest in her.

Matt had to admit, though, that her bad behavior wasn't entirely her fault. He'd spoiled Onika and turned her into the ornery, demanding monster she'd become.

"Here you go." Onika handed Puddin a set of keys. "Apartment 10. Go on in and make yourself at home. There's a little bit of food in the fridge." Onika nodded toward Matt. "This asshole's been bringing me stuff to snack on instead of taking me to the supermarket to do some real grocery shopping."

Matt wanted to defend himself and explain to Onika that with all the furniture shopping they'd done and having to hold down two jobs, he hadn't had the time to take her shopping for groceries. But he didn't dare disagree with Onika. He sat quietly with his head in his hands.

"But I got a little something, something…enough ham and cheese slices to make yourself a couple sandwiches."

"Ham and cheese!" Laughing, Puddin rubbed her plump tummy. "You ain't gotta tell me twice."

"You crazy, girl," Onika replied. "I'm gon sit in the van for a minute. Me and this dickhead gotta have a private conversation."

"Aiight. Holla if you need me," Puddin said, narrowing an eye at Matt.

"So what's the deal with you?" Onika asked Matt after Puddin waddled off.

"Nothing," Matt muttered.

"Nigga please. What's your problem? Spit it out before I smack the shit outta you," she said, raising her hand.

Without a doubt, Matt could physically put a hurting on skinny little Onika if he chose to. But her emotional hold on him was so intense, he feared her. He was afraid of loosing the woman whose mistreatment of him served as an aphrodisiac—the woman whose vaginal juices invigorated him like a double dose of Viagra. Matt took a deep breath. "Actually, there is something wrong. For one thing, I wish you wouldn't talk to me with such blatant disrespect when other people are around. It's degrading and I don't appreciate it." Matt took a deep breath and continued. "And secondly, I really wish you wouldn't put your—"

"Secondly, my ass!" Onika gripped Matt by the collar. "I don't give a shit about what you wish!" She tightened her grip and pulled Matt closer, so close, he could feel her warm breath on his face. "Don't make me bash your fuckin' head against that window," she threatened and then released him with a hard shove.

Matt felt the hardening inside his pants. His eyes locked helplessly on Onika's face.

Recognizing the desire that shone in his eyes, Onika patted Matt's crotch and then ran an open palm across the small bulge beneath the fabric. "Aw, my boo might not have to eat no pussy tonight," she said with a smile. "Looks like you're ready to get your fuck on." Onika tenderly stroked the cheek she'd bruised a few minutes ago.

Boo! Matt's heart soared. He'd been feeling insecure lately, but those emotions evaporated as Onika caressed his cheek with one hand and massaged his penis with the other. She couldn't help it if at times her bad temper got out of control. His poor little baby girl had had a hard life. Something really awful must have happened to her while she was out on the streets, he reasoned.

"Come on, Mr. Wheeler. Let's go in the crib so you can put some dick up in this pussy—like a real man."

∾

Matt tried to fuck Onika like a real man, but he couldn't. On the air mattress inside Onika's empty bedroom, Matt's manhood had deflated the moment it touched Onika's pussy. "I can't understand it," he mumbled, pulling desperately on his limp penis. "I'm sorry, baby. You're gonna have to sit on my face until I get myself together," he said, regretfully.

"I'm not sitting on nothing but the driver's seat of your van. You're getting on my damn nerves." Onika stood up and held out her hand. "Give me the keys to your van," she demanded.

"Don't be like that, Onika," Matt pleaded. "Come on, baby girl, let me give you some head. Don't you want to cum all over daddy's face?"

"No! I want to cum on a goddamn dick. You got me frustrated," Onika complained as she snatched Matt's pants off the floor and shook his key ring out of a side pocket. "I'm starting to really wonder about you. Whassup, you gay or something, Mr. Wheeler?"

"No!" Matt said vehemently. "You know I'm not a homosexual."

Onika shrugged. "So you say." Dangling Matt's key ring, she added, "I thought you were gonna serve up some hard dick tonight, but it seems like all you wanna do is tongue me to death."

Matt looked miserable. "I thought you enjoyed oral sex with me. Please, baby girl, sit on my face," Matt pleaded and then reached for Onika's hand.

Onika jerked her hand from Matt's. "Puddin!" she shouted at the top of her lungs.

Puddin hustled to the bedroom and burst through the door, clutching an unusually thick ham and cheese sandwich with mayonnaise oozing out the sides. "Did he hit you?" Puddin asked, balling her fists.

"Nah, I do all the hitting in this relationship," Onika boasted. "I need a favor."

"A favor? Girl, I thought you was in here being manhandled. Why you screaming my name while I'm trying to get a grub?" Puddin took a bite of the sandwich and licked a dollop of mayonnaise from her finger. Preoccupied with her appetite, she didn't seem to notice or care that Onika and Matt were naked.

But Matt cared. He was mortified that Onika and her friend were having a casual conversation as if he weren't on the air mattress butt-ass-naked. He desperately wanted to cover his exposed genitals with the sheet. He placed a hand over his private parts and eyed his Eagles cap, wishing it was on his head, concealing his receding hairline. When they'd first entered the bedroom—when Onika's mood was lighter because she thought he'd be able to maintain an erection—she had playfully yanked the cap off Matt's head. Before Matt could stop her, she'd flung his Eagles cap across the room.

"Mr. Wheeler wants to get a grub, too!" Onika announced.

Completely perplexed, both Matt and Puddin stared at Onika.

"Mr. Wheeler got the hots for you," Onika explained.

I do not! Matt shouted in his mind. But he knew better than to contradict Onika out loud.

"He was checking out your big ass when you got out of the van."

Puddin blushed. "Get outta here. You lying?"

"I'm not lying. Mr. Wheeler wants to eat your pussy. Don't you, boo." Teasingly, Onika elbowed Matt, causing the hand that shielded his personals to slip away. Horrified at Onika's suggestion, Matt was too stunned to speak and too shocked to care about his penis.

"Dayum! Where's the rest of his dick?" Puddin' blurted and then cracked up in laughter. Red-faced with embarrassment, Matt immediately clamped both hands over his penis.

"It's small right now, but it'll grow a couple more inches when it gets hard. But you ain't gotta worry about him trying to use it. He don't wanna fuck nobody but me. I gotta make a quick run. I need you to feed him some pussy so he can stay hard 'til I get back."

Puddin giggled. "Y'all crazy, but aiight. I'll do it. You know me, I ain't never turned down no food or no opportunity to get my pussy ate," Puddin replied with a big, cheesy grin. She clenched the sandwich between her teeth as she unhooked the chain that dangled through the loops of her jeans.

Puddin looked so disgusting with the sandwich hanging out of her mouth that Matt felt compelled to put his foot down and stand up to Onika. "Onika!" he said firmly, "What the hell is wrong with you. I'm not—"

Before Matt could utter another word, Onika drew her hand back and sent a stinging slap across his face. His hands went to his face, defensively

"See what I mean, Puddin?" Onika remarked, attempting to explain her violent response. "Do you see how I gotta keep him in check?" Breathing hard, Onika shook her head. "Dealing with this nigga is hard work."

"I can see that," Puddin agreed, sympathetically. Neglecting to finish peeling off the too-tight jeans, she once again attacked the ham and cheese sandwich, while watching in fascination as Matt's small dick quivered and sprang to life.

Onika smiled down at her accomplishment. "Tough love! That's all my boo needs," Onika bragged. She scowled at Puddin. "Damn, girl. Hurry up and get outta those jeans. You gotta squat over Mr. Wheeler and keep him occupied while I make my run."

"I'm moving as fast as I can. But I'm a big girl—it takes me a minute to struggle out of my clothes."

Finally stripped naked, Puddin maneuvered over and straddled Matt's face and pressed her pussy against his unwilling mouth while she munched happily on her swiftly dwindling sandwich.

Allowing himself to be debased by Onika and her fat friend was disgusting and arousing at the same time, and he felt his penis stiffen. It was hard enough to slip inside Onika. He was sure of it. But Onika, dressing quickly, had other plans.

"Suck her pussy real good, boo," Onika said with affection as she strolled out of the bedroom.

With Onika's blessings, Puddin enthusiastically rotated her pussy against Matt's unwilling lips. Mayonnaise dripped from her sandwich, dotting Matt's forehead as well as the air mattress he lay upon.

THE RAW ESSENTIALS OF HUMAN SEXUALITY

BY D.V. BERNARD

The old man drove like an old man: slowly—as though he could not possibly have a destination in mind. Other cars passed them, honking angrily. Morton glanced over at the old man and saw there was a content, far-off expression on his face. He was about to ask the old man what he was so happy about, but then thought better of it. He went back to staring out of the window. They were driving around downtown Orlando now. Several times, the old man went in circles, so that Morton became convinced he was lost. Eventually, the old man looked over at him:

"Do you know anything about tantric sex?"

Morton looked over at him confusedly. "About what?"

"Tantric sex: an Oriental view of sex. It came out of yoga and Hinduism and so on. ...Men believed they could drain off female energy through sex. They figured the more pleasure they gave a woman, the more of her energy they received."

Morton stared at him. He found himself smiling: "You believe in it?"

"I think there might be some merit to it," he drawled. "…You ever just sit back and observe sex? I don't mean fake porn sex: orchestrated images of how people wished they fucked. I'm talking the raw essentials: the real deal. [Morton was looking at him confusedly, wary of where this entire conversation might lead.] I suggest you look into it when you get the chance," the old man suggested. "The true nature of human sexuality is not what people think."

Morton had been looking on uneasily, but at that comment, he smiled. "What is it then?"

"Sex is the true vehicle of God's power." The old man's face was so earnest that Morton did not know whether to be amused, disturbed or respectful—the way one was supposed to be respectful of all religious views. When Ferguson saw his anxious stare, he smiled. "You would benefit greatly from my wisdom, young buck."

Morton laughed. "What do you think you have to share, old man?" he said playfully.

"I've figured out the raw essentials of human sexuality." The old man's statement was so bombastic that Morton could not help but laugh. Yet, even though the old man smiled, his expression remained earnest.

"…I was thinking about my pappy just now," Ferguson began when Morton's laughter died down. "That's why I asked you if you believed in tantric sex. There was a rumor about him. He was in his nineties and still bedding these young girls: thirteen, fourteen…They said he would drain them—sustain himself with the sex."

Morton laughed uneasily. "You mean like some kind of sex vampire?"

The old man laughed. "I guess that's what you could call it. ...My momma died when I was a baby, so it was only my pappy and me. When I was about ten, he had this thirteen-year-old mistress. He got her from another town. He had this little house out back where he took his women. I'd hear those young girls screaming out from the sex. Sometimes, they'd be screaming for an hour. My pappy had him a man-sized appetite," the old man mused with a proud grin. "...Like I was saying, when I was ten, I finally got the nerve to sneak out back and look in the window. My pappy was with that thirteen-year-old I mentioned. Compared to my pappy, she was just a twig: an itty-bitty thing. I hid in the bushes, so I could be right at the window when they started. The first thing he did was strip her—practically ripped off her clothes. Then he had her on that bed. Soon, she was screaming—"

Morton grimaced.

"Don't be so squeamish," the old man said with a laugh. "Anyway, when that girl started screaming, my first thought was that my pappy was too big for her...but it was more than that. My father was on top of her, but I could see her face, since they were lying at an angle to me. And it wasn't as if I was a horny kid taking a peek. While I stood there, it was like being in church: like seeing God's will being done. It scares you to be around that kind of power. You want to shield your eyes from it—like you want to shield your eyes from the sun. ...After a while, I swear my pappy's skin seemed to glow with God's power. He seemed energized—stronger, more youthful. Even that young girl seemed amazed by it. We were seeing God's will: bowing down before the altar of His true church—"

The old man laughed when he looked over and saw Morton's expression. "You don't look too good, boy."

"I don't feel well," Morton conceded.

"Well, you should be back in bed. I told you to stay in my room," Ferguson reminded him. "…But I guess if you hadn't been there tonight, those young punks might have done me some harm."

Morton grunted noncommittally. Looking out of the windshield, he saw they were stopping in front of a seedy-looking bar. By the looks of things, they were on the outskirts of town. The old man parked and looked over at him, still smiling:

"A good stiff drink will fix us both up: make us as good as new."

Morton shrugged, and they both exited the car. Morton felt lightheaded as he stood up. He rested against the car for a few seconds, but moved on when the old man looked over at him, since he did not want to talk about how he felt. The bar was a real dive. The lighting was low; the stools and chairs were upholstered with neon green vinyl, and the entire place smelled of beer, urine and vomit. At this relatively early hour, only a handful of dour men sat at the bar, their faces morose and distant. The old man gestured to a booth, and they sat down. The seat was sticky when they sat, and the tabletop was littered with shelled peanuts. Morton looked around again, then up at the old man, as if to ask him why he would come into such a place.

"This, here, is a real drinking man's bar," Ferguson explained. "Sometimes a man needs to be a man. You go into some of these bars, and it's as if it's some kind of tea party. You come to a place like this, and you can practically smell the manhood."

Morton chuckled. "I definitely smell something."

A waitress in a skimpy outfit came over, but she seemed drained—as if all her life's dreams had already been dashed. She tried to smile—since smiling at men in bars was the way for waitresses to get good tips—but her face remained grim.

The old man ordered two beers. Morton wished he had not come. The bar was depressing. If this place was a true reflection of manhood then they were all doomed.

"Were you ever married?" the old man asked him now.

"No."

"Really? Never had a special woman in your life?"

"Nah, I spent half my life in the Marines."

"That keeps a man from finding a good woman?"

Morton laughed. "Not at all. When the Military sends you all over the world, you find good women everywhere you go."

Ferguson smiled. The waitress came back with the beer. The old man paid her and gave her a fat tip. Her face brightened. When she was gone, he said, "See how easy it was to make her day? In a place like this, everything is simple."

"You like simplicity, huh?"

"Definitely. For an old man like me, nothing is simple—even taking a shit." He laughed, and Morton could not help but join in. Afterwards, he drank down half the beer. He was beginning to hope he would have a quick drink and then head back, but the old man called the waitress over and ordered a pitcher of beer. She came eagerly; this time, her smile was genuine.

"She reminds me of my wife," the old man said when she was gone. Morton looked over at him cautiously. The old man continued: "My wife is a real beauty. ...She wasn't more than sixteen the first time I laid eyes on her."

Despite himself, Morton observed: "I guess both you and your daddy liked them young."

The old man laughed out. "It ain't what you think. ...But she was a real beauty. I was dedicating a library in a small town in Alabama. ...Dirt poor town. I paid for the library: all the books, everything. I've been to countless charity ceremonies like that, full of dignitaries and politicians: people who want to be around power. But she was there this time: young and beautiful and full of life. I knew right away she had something special. She had everything I needed." There was a hungry expression on the old man's face; Morton looked away uneasily. In his mind's eye, he saw Ferguson making love to the wife: her smooth, brown skin pressed against the old man's wrinkled, liver-spotted flesh. When he cringed, the old man laughed apologetically. "You must think I'm some old pervert: a depraved old white man, preying on a sweet young black thang."

Morton feigned disinterest: "It's not for me to judge."

The old man smiled at his attempt at diplomacy. Remembering he had her picture in his wallet, he took it out and stretched his hand out across the table. "There she is," Ferguson announced, holding the picture before Morton's eyes. "Tell me if any man with blood flowing through his veins would be able to resist her."

Morton looked at the picture anxiously, then returned to his drink. "She's very beautiful," he said flatly.

The old man laughed in amazement: "You're acting as though I just showed you baby pictures of my ugly brat. *Look*, at her. Look at her *good*, and tell me she ain't perfection." The old man moved the picture closer, so that his scent of death and disease flared in Morton's nostrils—

"She's beautiful, okay," he said, growing more anxious by the second. "What do you want me to say?" he went on. "I'm happy for you, okay? You have a wife any man would love to have. Is that what you wanted me to say?"

The old man sniggered. "I wasn't trying to brag. I only wanted you to understand how I felt when I saw her that first time. She had everything I needed. And in her eyes, there was a hunger."

"A hunger for what?"

"For life. She was perfection, itself. When I saw her that first time, I had the same feeling I had when I saw my pappy with that young girl. My wife was something to be praised. I felt God's energy flowing through her, and I knew I wasn't ready."

Morton wanted to get away from this entire conversation. "Well," he started sarcastically, "I guess everything worked out, since you got her to marry you."

"It would appear that way, but things are not always as they seem." When Morton looked at him confusedly, the old man continued: "What if I told you I've never made love to my wife."

Morton frowned.

The old man laughed again. "It ain't what you're thinking. You see an old man like me and you figure I can't get my rod up no more. As old as I am, you figure my dick ain't good for nothing but keeping my balls warm."

Morton laughed. The old man concluded:

"I may not be a young thoroughbred like you, but I can still get around the racetrack."

"I'm happy for you," he said with a smile. But then, as the old man's words registered in his mind again, he sobered. "Then why haven't you been with your wife?"

"I'm still not ready."

Morton chuckled. "You'd better hurry up, old man, before you run out of time. If your wife means as much to you as you say, seems you'd be with her every chance you got. You almost seem scared of her."

"I *am* scared of her. I ain't afraid to admit it."

Morton frowned, intrigued. "What are you afraid *of*?"

"If you pluck a flower, it dies, and it loses all its beauty."

"What does that have to do with it? She's a woman—not a flower." The beer had loosened Morton up, so that he added, "You've convinced yourself your wife's going to break if you touch her. She ain't a Ming vase that you've gotta worry about smashing. Hiding from her ain't gonna do you any good. You get your value out of a woman by using her: by doing things to her," he said with an insinuating smile.

"What's the longest you ever went without sex?" the old man asked abruptly.

"…I guess when I was in the war: about nine months."

"I've been married for four years and I ain't had sex with her yet."

"Damn, what are you waiting for?"

"Timing is everything. I've got to wait for the right time and conditions."

The entire scenario had Morton laughing again. "What about your wife? She don't mind waiting?"

Ferguson smiled faintly. "Make no mistake about it: I know my wife has her womanly needs. Indeed, I know she has a lover."

It took all Morton's willpower not to leap out of his skin. He forced himself to look over at the man and maintain eye contact. "How'd you know that?"

"Like I said, I've been around the racetrack a few times. I'm aware of what goes on in my own house." He said this last part with a nonchalant wave of his hand, but his eyes were sharp.

Morton felt suddenly sick and weak. He forced himself to talk again: "What are you going to do about your wife?"

"You mean her cheating?"

Morton nodded.

"It really doesn't concern me."

Morton looked at him in bewilderment. "You don't care that another man is taking what's yours?"

"Ah, but that's the thing: he's not taking anything. Maybe he's too stupid to realize he's not ready for my wife either." He was smiling.

Morton shook his head: "I don't understand you at all, old man." Yet, as he said this, he grasped his head: he was feeling weaker and sicker by the second. He felt empty inside—hollowed out. It was as if he were being starved—as if he had not eaten in weeks. He remembered his face in the rear view mirror: how he had looked *old*—

"You don't look so good," the old man said, but there was a strange grin on his face. As Morton stared at it, it occurred to him his vision was getting blurry. That was when his body began to slump; within seconds, everything went black.

₭♥ℛ

Regaining consciousness was a slow process. In the beginning, he was aware only of noises: jumbled words and the far-off groan of a car engine. Even after Morton opened his eyes, his mind was unable to decode what was going on around him. Everything was blurry and dark—

"Look, he's waking up." It was a woman's voice. Morton tried to focus his eyes, but it was pointless—

"Never mind him," another voice responded to the woman, "—just do what I'm paying you to do." Morton's mind was still sputtering along, but after a few seconds, he realized it was Ferguson's voice! As always, the drawl triggered a rampaging terror within him. Pieces of the previous scene flashed in his mind: talking at the bar; Ferguson grinning as he passed out... He began to panic: something sinister was taking place about him. He felt the certainty in his soul. He willed his eyes to focus. It took as long as a minute, but eventually, he made out a woman's form. She was on top of him, straddling him. Initially, her head seemed monstrously huge and grotesque; but then, as she leaned forward, he saw it was only a wig. He stared at her in his dazed, semi-conscious state. The sensation reminded him of the time when he was sixteen, and some guys on his block tricked him into smoking a PCP-laced joint. His mother had died the previous month. One of his mother's great aunts had taken him in, but the old lady's superstitions and bible-thumping ways had only driven him to the streets. He had needed something to belong to. Unfortunately for him, the neighborhood hustlers and thugs had been in a malicious mood that day. They had taken him to the local park, and offered him the joint. After a few drags, he had started feeling dizzy. Soon, they had been laughing at him as he lay on the ground, barely able to lift his head. They had kicked him and pissed on him, and rubbed dog shit on him...but when he woke up an hour or so later, besmeared and defiled, he had taken his revenge with a baseball bat. He had beaten the first two into near comas before the police tracked him down. They had found him walking the streets, his clothes still smeared with dog feces and his victims' blood. Finding PCP in his system, they had sent him to a juvenile prison that specialized in drug rehabilitation. There, he had spent two years with heroin addicts and other youths who had committed violent crimes while high. He had joined the Marines right after he was released. Typically, the Military would have rejected an application from a drug felon, but there had been a war on, his drug test had been clean, and the counselors from the rehabilitation center had vouched for his "moral character."

Morton remembered it all as he looked up in a daze and saw the woman straddling him. She was young—maybe eighteen at the most. He had been concentrating on her face, to see if he knew her, but as he glanced down, he saw they were both naked. Her breasts were pert and perfect. He stared at them as if in a trance—

"He's not even hard," the girl protested.

The response was immediate and gruff: "Then put your mouth on him, gal!"

Morton looked to the left for the first time—to where the old man's voice was coming. There was initially only a shadow there; but after a few moments, the old man leaned forward, so that his face was highlighted by the streetlamp outside. It was only then that Morton realized they were all in a car. He and the woman were in the back of Ferguson's luxury rental; the old man was in the front, looking back at them with an eager grin on his face.

"Handle your business, gal," the old man encouraged her; a few seconds later, Morton's body tensed as her warm, wet tongue began manipulating his penis. He looked to see her head bobbing up and down. Her massive wig impeded his view. The old man must have been thinking the same thing, because he wrenched off the wig at that moment. Underneath, her hair was short and boyish—but she seemed like a real person at last. She glanced up at him. In the darkness, he could not see her eyes. For a moment, he thought there might be nothing there but empty sockets. ...But her head was still bobbing up and down. The sloppy sounds of a blowjob had always turned him on. Despite everything, he groaned.

He became aware his penis was fully erect—which was miraculous, since the rest of his body was still numb and lethargic. His body seemed to be fading into the nothingness—disappearing into the surrounding darkness. Somehow, his erect penis anchored him to this plane of existence. All his strength seemed concentrated on his shaft—

"He looks good and stiff now, gal," Ferguson pointed out. The girl seemed lost in performing her sloppy fellatio, because she only moaned her accent. After a few seconds, the old man became exasperated with her, and screamed, "Sit on that goddamn cock, gal! I ain't paying you for no lip action!"

In his dazed state, maybe it was only then Morton realized she was a prostitute. The girl looked up at the old man in annoyance, then she grabbed her purse from off the floor and retrieved a condom. She was about to rip the package open when the old man stopped her:

"Hell, no! For all I'm paying you, you'd better ride him bareback."

"I ain't trying to catch no diseases," the girl protested.

"Then you're in the wrong goddamn profession!" the old man cursed her. When the girl seemed on the verge of reconsidering everything, the old man added: "If he's screwing my own wife, then he's safe enough to screw you."

The girl looked up at him, confused. "You say he's fucking your wife?"

"That's what I said. Now, stop wasting time, and jump up on that dick. I'll throw in an extra five hundred dollars for you."

Talk of money piqued her interest: "Where it at?"

The old man groaned and took out his wallet. He retrieved five crisp hundred dollar bills and handed them to her. She snatched them out of his hand, then held them up to the light outside, apparently making sure they were real. When she was convinced, a wide grin came over her face. Through all this, Morton remained dazed. He did not fully hear the words; and even if he had, he would not have been able to do anything about them.

The girl shoved the bills in her purse, then she zipped it closed, as if she feared the bills would fall out. Next, she straddled Morton once more, and grabbed the base of his penis. She stroked it a few times, to make sure it was still fully erect—

The old man laughed out as he saw the girl was ready. Suddenly jovial, Ferguson reached out and patted Morton on the shoulder, saying, "You're about to experience it now, boy: the raw essentials!"

Morton gasped as the girl impaled herself on his penis. As a Military man, he had had his fair share of prostitutes. His Military career had been a twelve-year sex romp, interspersed with the horror of war and the boredom of being trapped on distant bases with nothing to do. Throughout the world, prostitutes had one motive: to get their johns to reach orgasm quickly, so that they could dispense with them as quickly as possible. A good prostitute did not need more than thirty seconds to a minute. The girl riding Morton had her teeth bared, as if she were a wild animal. The inside of her was warm and tight, and velvety soft. She clenched the muscles of her vagina rhythmically. Morton groaned. He felt the ridges of her inner walls; as she rammed her hips down on him, he felt her cervix stabbing the head of his penis. He groaned again—half in pain and half from the exquisite pleasure.

The old man laughed out. "It won't be too much longer now, boy! I found a nice young, tight one for you, didn't I?"

Morton's eyes darted up. The old man was leering at him, his yellowish teeth highlighted by the streetlamp outside. The sight was ghoulish, but Morton felt the orgasmic pleasure building up in his belly. In the background, the old man's laugh was grating against his nerves. His muscles clenched; where there had before been numbness, he now felt raw, surging power. And then, all at once, he was in the midst of it, shuddering as his seed sprayed the walls of her vagina. On top of him, even the girl was screaming. He looked up at her face then. It was contorted—*monstrous*. After a moment of confusion, he realized the power he had felt coursing through his body was still building. Instead of a post-orgasmic release, there was an explosive escalation of the power. The pleasure was perfect—as if he had reached a new plane of existence. On top of him, the girl was still screaming; her face, when he saw it, seemed disfigured: mangled. Her body was convulsing now; and as much as he wanted to believe her convulsions came from pleasure, he knew terror when he saw it. She was trying to get away from him; her arms flailed, beating his chest, but it was as if some force were compelling her to continue grinding against his penis. The sight was horrific, but by then the pleasure had escalated to the point where Morton was blissfully unaware of his surroundings. …Soon, the girl's body began to cave in. Her young, smooth skin began to wrinkle and droop; her eyes lost their luster and her hair began to gray; but through it all, Morton was far away from it all. Indeed, by the time the girl's decaying husk slid from his penis, he was like a god soaring in the heavens.

ANOTHER TIME, ANOTHER PLACE

ZANE

NOVEMBER 12, 1986

Dear Diary,

His dick was curved. Not a huge curve but curved just enough to work my pussy in all the right spots. When a man's dick is too straight, it can be painful. A sister needs a brother to be able to move with her groove. I remember my ex-boyfriend, Tony. His dick was like a wooden plank. It would not budge for anything and even when I tried to get on top and maneuver to get some serious action going, it was too much damn work. He would leave me sick, unsatisfied and feeling like I had gone through an OB/GYN examination with that duck lips tool.

Back to the one with the curved dick. I licked it last night, like it was the most delicious chocolate ice cream cone in the world. No, not a cone, a Popsicle with chocolate on the outside and vanilla cream on the inside. I wanted that cream, too. I wanted him to shoot it down my throat like a human geyser. I wanted him to cum so much that I could gargle with his sperm. I know all this sounds nasty but I am simply a woman who loves dick. Now the men that dicks are attached to are another question. There is Darrell. He's nice enough. We met at the grocery store the other day. He seems like a brother who is about something other than trying to see how many pairs of panties he can get into. We will have to wait and see what happens.

Anyway, back to last night. I was standing on a balcony, the wind blowing the curtains outward and teasing my hair as I overlooked the skyline. I could sense his presence as he walked—no, glided—up behind me. I could smell his cologne. Mmm, he smelled like heaven. He was wearing all white. A doubled-breasted suit with no shirt. His chest was chiseled, like the rest of him. His skin was moistened—his deep dark skin. His bald head was shaved smooth, like his face, and his thick lips encased perfectly straight white teeth.

"Did you miss me?" he whispered in my ear, after joining me on the balcony.

I could not answer. I only managed a whimper. My entire body, from the soles of my feet to the tips of my fingers to the baby-fine hair of my pussy was calling out his name. Strange as this is, I still do not know his name. I know every inch of his body, his voice; his dick, but not his name.

He comes to me every night now, no matter what city I am in, no matter what time zone. I cannot wait to get through the performances at work so I can rush to be with him. Our favorite fucking song is "Do Me Baby" by Prince, followed by "Fire and Desire" by Rick James and Teena Marie. Both of those songs make me so fucking hot. My pussy stays drenched from merely thinking about being with him. Once we are together, we ignite. I am surprised the bed has not caught fire from all the serious fucking we engage in.

He always gives me a serious dick down and I do mean dick down. I can hear the sound of his balls slapping up against me as I type this. Mmm, damn, I wish he was inside me right now. I wish that I was sitting on his dick, with my back to him, rocking back and forth as I sit here at my computer. A sister can get a lot of work done that way. When he fucks me, a feeling comes over me that I cannot quite express. I shiver, but I feel calm at the same time. No man has ever made me feel so desired, like he is so pleased by my efforts.

He eats my pussy until I detonate all over his tongue. It is such an amazing feeling. I only wish that I could fuck him twenty-four seven, but life intervenes. If I could, I would walk around with his dick in my ass; in my pussy; in my mouth. Ooh, yes, definitely in my mouth.

Damn, I am getting fired up just writing this. I hope he comes back tonight so we can "cum together" and fornicate under the consent of the king. I know he'll be here. I need to go bathe and get ready for him, so he can bury his dick into me balls deep and put me to sleep like a baby.

Kisses,

Kiss

NEGRIL, JAMAICA
SEPTEMBER 1987

ALECK

"Man, there are a ton of fine women over here," Mike said to me as we headed to the beach in the late afternoon. "We should have had our asses over here years ago."

"You are such a pussy hound." I swatted him on the back with my beach towel. "We're here to relax and take a break from a hectic work schedule. Not to get laid."

"Shit, you might not be here to get laid, but I am. If I don't get pussy every day, I feel sick. It's my medicine. It keeps me alive. I'm trying to see as much pink meat as I can before we head back next week."

"You are so damn nasty. Better watch out with these Jamaican women. You might try to fuck one that has a man slinging a machete. Then the only color you'll be seeing is red and I'll be carrying your body back in a bag. Imagine that, me having to explain that you got murdered in Jamaica because you were trolling for pussy in another man's marked territory."

Mike waved me off and started flexing his muscles. "Aleck, please. I know how to handle any motherfucking thing that comes my way. If a man can't fuck his woman good enough to keep her at home, that's his damn issue. Women don't cheat when they're satisfied."

"That's complete bullshit," I said. "Men can have the best woman in the world. Perfect in every way and some will still cheat."

"The key word was *satisfied*." Mike glared at me. "A real man is never satisfied. Not when there are more varieties to be sampled." He pointed in the direction of three women sitting on lounge chairs near the tip of the ocean. "Speaking of which… Damn, check them hookers out."

"What makes you think they're hookers?" Mike really disgusted me sometimes with the way he referred to women. I glanced at the women and all of them were drop-dead gorgeous. "They don't look Jamaican. They're probably vacationing here from the States; like us."

"That's even better. We can fuck them over here and then collect some more ass when we get back stateside. I have a shit load of frequent flyer miles. I hope they live in one of the cities where Delta flies. "

I chuckled. "I see that you've got it all figured out."

Mike rubbed his chin and gloated. "I always do, my man."

"What about Candace?"

"Who?" Mike asked sarcastically.

"Candace? Your wife?"

"Oh, her…" Mike sighed. "Look, Aleck. I realize you think that I'm wrong for cheating on Candace, but she knew what she was getting when she walked down the aisle. I'm a man and men are going to do what men do. Candace saw that writing all over the wall. Shit, I practically spelled it out for her. Like most women, she decided that my feelings were more important than her self-respect and I ain't mad at her. She wanted a husband, a bad crib, kids, all that. She has it and as long I'm paying all the bills, I can do whatever the hell I want."

I shook my head. "I don't believe in cheating. I believe in karma. When I do find Mrs. Right, I don't want my past catching up to me."

"Yeah, well, that's you. I am an All-American man and I will not live my life dedicated to one pussy—not even if it's made out of Kryptonite."

There was no use in continuing that discussion. Mike was not going to miraculously grow a conscience; not in Jamaica with half-naked women everywhere. If we were at a convention of convents, Mike would try to fuck a bunch of nuns who had sworn off sex. He was convinced he could talk any woman into spreading her legs.

Besides, he was right. Candace realized what she was getting into. Mike disrespected her time and time again while they were dating. Despite everyone warning her to move on, she was determined to get him down the aisle. Sure, on the surface he was a good man, a good provider. The ugly truth was hidden underneath the fancy six-bedroom home, the Jaguar and Mercedes, and the limitless spending sprees Candace got to enjoy.

Even though the sun was about to go down, the sand was still piping hot between my toes. "Damn, it's hot out here."

"We're in Jamaica, Fool," Mike said, continuing the topic I had decided to drop. "And don't even go there about cheating. You've cheated plenty of times. You forget; we go way back."

"Exactly—way back. I cheated on sisters in college but I have outgrown that since then. I believe in honesty and if I'm not feeling a woman enough to be with her and only her, then I tell her straight up and let her make an informed decision."

Mike laughed. "Maybe that's why you don't currently have a woman. Fuck that honesty nonsense. Women can't handle the truth."

I hated to admit it to myself, but Mike did have a somewhat valid point. Every time I tried to tell a woman that I was feeling her but not yet in love, she would get offended. All the women that I met tended to want to go from casual dating to shacking up or getting engaged in less than six months. At the age of 29, I had only had one close brush with marriage but Brenda decided that she wanted to get back with her high school sweetheart. That practically destroyed my faith in women, but I continued to date—in protect mode.

It had been hard for anyone to break down that barrier for nearly seven years. I had doubts that I would find a woman who could be my complete package. Then we walked up on those three women so Mike could make his move and the one in the red bikini instantly made me think twice.

KISS

My heart skipped a beat; then it fluttered. It was the man from my fantasies—all my sexual fantasies. The one with the curved dick. He was wearing black swim trunks and walking toward us with another man in a blue pair. They were both attractive, but the one in the black…I couldn't believe it was really him.

"Humph, do you see what I see?" Nancy whispered and then poked me and Calibri in the arms, in that order. She was sitting between us but she sat up slightly so she could get a better look. "Here comes some of that Jamaican Mandingo meat."

Calibri giggled. "They don't look Jamaican, but they do look damn scrumptious. I hope they're single."

Nancy said, "I don't care if they're single or married, as long as they're available to play with my kitty kat."

Calibri smacked her lips. "Nancy, we're here to relax. One last week of girl fun before the big day. We didn't come here to get fucked."

"Speak for your damn self," Nancy replied. "Ain't nothing wrong with fucking as long as it's good. It's been two weeks since I rode, sucked, or intook any dick and that ain't good. I'm used to getting some at least twice a week."

"No one wants to know your fucking schedule," Calibri said. "Two weeks is nothing. Some sisters go years because they refuse to have a lousy fuck…or a casual one."

"Well, crucify me then," Nancy said. "I'm living this life once and I'm going to do what the hell I want to do. We all have separate rooms. What goes on in mine is my business."

"True that," Calibri agreed. "Thank goodness for it, too. I wouldn't be able to stomach seeing you fuck or, heaven forbid, listen to you slobber all over some man's dick."

I did not say a word. I was still in a state of euphoria while they went back and forth with each other. For nearly a year, I had been experiencing these crazy fantasies and masturbating myself into a frenzy over a man in my dreams—the one now walking in the sand less than a hundred feet away.

As they got closer, Nancy started smoothing down her short hair and repositioning her tits in her white crocheted bikini top. "I want the one in the black. No, the one in the blue. Shit, I'm undecided."

Calibri said, "Calm yourself down. For all you know, they might not even want you."

Nancy got offended and glared at Calibri. "What man wouldn't want all this?"

Nancy had recently gotten a breast augmentation and had gone from 36Cs to 36DDDs and you could not tell her that she was not God's gift to man.

"Hello, ladies," the one in the blue trunks said as they grew nearer. "Enjoying yourselves out on this lovely beach?"

"Things are definitely looking better," Nancy said, jumping up and extending her hand. "Hey, I'm Nancy."

The guy took her hand and kissed her knuckles. "I'm Mike." He pointed to his friend, with whom I had made eye contact; we were staring each other down. "This is my buddy, Aleck."

Mike was about five feet nine inches, light-skinned with amber eyes and a great build. But he was not my type. Aleck was around six feet four inches, dark as midnight and bald and he had the darkest, most alluring eyes. *Damn, he was definitely the man from my dreams.*

Nancy pushed her breasts out at Mike. He seemed disinterested in them and pointed at Calibri and me. "Are these your friends?"

After sighing and making a show of it by putting her hands on her hips, Nancy said, "Yes, we're from Los Angeles. And you?"

"We're from the D.C. area," Mike said.

It did not escape any of us that she did not bother giving our names so Calibri chimed in. "I'm Calibri and that's Kiss."

"Kiss?!" the one named Aleck exclaimed, still staring at me. "As in K-I-S-S?"

"Yes," I replied, getting up off my lounger and brushing the sand off me. "My daddy said he fell in love with my mother during their first kiss, so it's kind of an inside joke."

Aleck looked my body up and down. I was doing the same damn thing to his. "Well, it's a nice joke. I've never met someone named Kiss before. It's definitely unique."

Calibri had stood up, without me even noticing it, until she rested her arm on my shoulder. "Kiss is a unique woman all around. Tell him what you do for a living," she urged.

Mike looked at me with interest then. "What do you do, Kiss?"

I knocked Calibri's arm off my shoulder. "I hate you." We both laughed. "I'm a clown and I'm proud of it."

"A clown?!" the two men exclaimed in unison.

"Yes, as in a circus clown," I stated, used to that reaction from people. "It's a family tradition."

"Both of her parents are with the circus," Nancy said, like it was a crime. "Her dad is the ringmaster and her mother is a trapeze artist."

"Wow, I didn't know that there were many black people in…" Mike started to say.

I interrupted him. "There are not that many, but it's what I do. Got a problem with it?"

Aleck crossed his arms and smiled. He was too fine. "I think it's cool."

"Baby, if you like it, I love it!" Mike yelled out. "As fine as you are, I bet you look sexy as all get out in a clown suit. I've never gotten it on with a clown before."

"No, you just act like one every time you open your mouth," Aleck remarked.

"Whatever, Man." Mike shot him a wicked look. "So, are you ladies busy this evening?"

"I'm available." Nancy moved closer to him to make sure he understood the ramifications of her statement.

He seemed turned off. "What about you, Calibri and Kiss?"

Calibri responded, "We don't have any major plans. We were going to dine by the water back at our hotel."

"Where you staying?" Aleck asked. "We're at the Ritz-Carlton."

"So are we," I said. "Great place."

"It's off the chain," Aleck added.

There was definitely chemistry between us. Little did he know that I had already fucked him in my imagination hundreds of times. My eyes dropped to his swim trunks, trying to figure out if his dick was curved.

ALECK

A clown named Kiss, I thought as I showered and prepared for an evening of promise. The only down side was that she was from Los Angeles and I resided in Washington, D.C.—a recent implant from Atlanta. *Since she's with a circus, that has to mean she travels constantly, which could be an up side or a down side depending on how I look at it. Hopefully the circus heads East and I can see her often. On the flip side, she might be so tied up with work that she'll have no time for me. Then again, she is in Jamaica on vacation.*

"Stop it!" I warned myself out loud. "You just met the woman!"

I finished rinsing the lather off me, got out the shower and began to get dressed. I chose a white linen casual suit, no shirt, to show off my pectoral muscles, and a pair of black sandals. Mike had recently convinced me to start getting pedicures. He said that men with smooth feet and shiny, clipped nails turned women on. Since my feet had seen better days, I decided to get one biweekly a couple of months before we headed to Jamaica.

Kiss was fine. She was about five feet six inches and thick. I loved a woman who fit comfortably into a size fourteen. She had a flat stomach, but the hips, thighs and chest were on point enough to sport that red bikini. She had mocha skin, smooth like a baby's, and dark brown eyes. Yes, I was definitely feeling her—to the point where it almost frightened me. It was like déjà vu. Like I had known her some place before. That was crazy. I had experienced my share of one-night stands in my younger years, but I never would have forgotten her.

Mike, that fool, would forget a woman in a heartbeat. I was so embarrassed one night while we were clubbing on the D.C. water-front. He spotted a woman and walked to her, proclaiming, "You're going to have to help me out here. I remember the pussy but I don't remember the name."

I was so embarrassed, but surprisingly, instead of slapping the living daylights out of him, the woman laughed and seemingly found it flat-tering. For the next two minutes, Mike tossed out name after name until she finally revealed that she was Jackie. They flirted for a good thirty minutes before her friend, who obviously did not find the situ-ation amusing at all, said she was tired and ready to go. Mike got the digits—again—and then ended up fucking her the next night and never called her again.

I don't believe in being disrespectful to women, being that I come from a single-parent home and I have five sisters. If any man ever spoke to my mother or one of my sisters that way, they would be eating teeth mixed with blood. That was part of the reason why I was sort of stressing the upcoming dinner with Kiss and her friends. I wanted her—badly—but I did not want to come off the wrong way. I realize that a lot of people vacation in the islands to get laid, but that was not my purpose at all. Mike and I had been working on a crazy schedule for months, trying to lock down a merger deal with a competing corporation. We were the crème de la crème of financial analysts but we also put in a lot of hours.

The only jacked-up thing about meeting someone on vacation is that if you want to pursue something other than sex, it's difficult. Even though I had not been in a bona-fide relationship for a long time, I was already hoping for something long-term with Kiss. Never one to believe in the proverbial "love at first sight," I now found myself contemplating if that was actually possible.

Men do think differently from women, so I was already assuming that in order to see her again after we left Jamaica for our respective home towns, I would have to lay some sex on her that she would never forget. Otherwise, why would she even pursue it? Women can claim otherwise all they want, but ultimately, sex is an integral part of a relationship to them and they want a man who can blow their back out. I was going to have to prove myself worthy or forget about it.

Women might worry about their bodies when it comes time to have sex but men have a lot of worries. Will our dick be big enough for the sister? Will we even be able to get the damn thing up? Will we be able to perform over and over again? Will we have enough stamina to wear her out? Will we serve up better dick service than every man who came before us?

I finished dressing and went down the hallway to knock on Mike's door. He and Candace had been married for going on five years and had two sons. He stopped wearing his wedding ring by year two, claiming it was too tight, but that was a lie. Candace did not seem to care, as long as she could lay claim to having a husband and a family. Many women feel that way but they are selling themselves short. Mike would nail anything he could and I was not surprised when a Jamaican maid, half-clothed, opened his hotel room door instead of him.

"He be ready in a minute," she said with her accent, walking into a disheveled room that reeked of sex. "He in da bathroom."

I could make out the smell of soap, mixed with pussy from the bed, and was glad that Mike had at least washed his ass. He came prancing out of the bathroom a moment later, dressed in black linen pants and a tan island shirt.

"Let's roll, Man." He looked at the maid. "Honey, can you change my sheets and tidy up the room before you leave?" He rubbed her on the head, like she was a puppy. "Thanks, Ma."

"Me see you later?" she asked.

"We'll see," he said hesitantly. "I know where to find you, Sugar."

She grinned from ear to ear, thinking that Mike was going to lay up with her again during our vacation. There was zero chance of that. Mike was not looking for love. He was searching for pussy and either Calibri or Nancy was next on his list. I had made it perfectly clear to him that Kiss was off limits and that he better not even gaze in her direction. That was another thing that I felt badly about—her unsuspecting friends. I had been alive long enough to know that women often held men responsible for the actions of their friends. Rarely did it work the other way. I had dated plenty of women whose "associates" had dogged over one of my boys but I never made the women feel bad about it. Let a man dog out a sister and all his friends are immediately just as guilty.

Part of me wanted to convince Mike to simply go to dinner and not try to sleep with one of Kiss's friends, but he would never go for that. His mind was made up; more than likely on trying to bed Calibri. Mike did not like aggressive women and Nancy looked like she was ready to fuck both of us on sight. Mike liked the challenge of obtaining the pussy. Even that maid had probably played hard to get at first, but he had eventually gotten the drawers and now she had been tossed into the pile of past notions.

"That pussy was a nice appetizer—Caribbean Jerk Punany," Mike bragged as we descended on the elevator to meet the ladies in the lobby. "Now I'm ready for the main course—Los Angeles Cream Pie. I wonder if I can get a two-for-one deal tonight. Too bad they're leaving tomorrow. If I had until we leave next week, I most definitely would fuck them both. Tonight's going to be a challenge, but I'm up for it."

I smirked. "I seriously doubt that. You might not get any play at all, so don't be surprised. Haven't you had enough sex for one night?"

"Hell no!" Mike exclaimed. "If there was only one chick as an option, then I might not want to bang her again, but I'm always down for new meat."

"That's all women are to you, huh? Meat?" I shook my head. "Did you talk to your *wife*?"

"Yes, I damn sure did," he replied, "and she loves me to death, my sons are fine, and you can drop the guilt trip act. I'm enjoying myself and you know how I am. You need to take a note from my book and enjoy life."

"I do enjoy my life, Mike. I simply don't feel like my dick has to regulate my every move."

It was his turn to smirk at me. "Yeah, right. I saw the way you were looking at Kiss earlier. You know you want to salute her with your wing-wang tonight. If you play your cards right, you might get lucky." As the elevator doors opened, he added, "Damn, I wish that I could make it with a clown. That's a new one. I wonder if she wears a red rubber nose and a wig to bed. That shit makes me hot just thinking about it."

"You are truly sick," I said, then laughed, halfway turned on by the thought myself.

KISS

When they walked into the beachside restaurant, I wondered how a man could grow even finer within the span of a few hours.

Aleck had on this white linen suit that brought out the beauty of his dark skin. He smiled as they approached us and my black thong got wet. Then again, I had been wet all day. I had returned to my room and masturbated for an hour, fantasizing about him...being inbetween my thighs. I imagined him fingering my pussy and then staring at me as he licked his fingertips one by one. I imagined him flipping me on my stomach and eating me out from the back as I buried my head in the sheets and held on to the bedposts. Mmm, yes, it was something. The great thing about this particular fantasy was that I now had a name to go with the face, the body and the curved dick.

"Hey, ladies," Mike said once they arrived at our table. "I don't know what smells better, the food or the three of you." He sat down next to Calibri and sniffed her neck. "What's that scent called? Paradise?"

Calibri blushed. "Oh, you have mad game."

"Hello, Kiss...Nancy...Calibri," Aleck said and each word sounded poetic.

"Hey, Sexy," Nancy stated seductively. I shot her an evil glare. She would not even want to go there.

We sat in that restaurant for a good three hours, eating, laughing and drinking. That get-to-know you period. Nancy and Calibri started vying for Mike's attention but it was obvious that he was down to fuck one of them, or both. It didn't matter to him as long as he got some pussy. Definitely not my type of man, but Nancy and Calibri thought he was hot.

"Would you like to take a walk on the beach?" Aleck asked me out of the blue.

"Absolutely." I quickly got up to follow him.

"Be good, or be good at it!" Nancy yelled out after us.

As we walked toward the shoreline, Aleck took my hand and nothing had ever felt so natural.

"Your friend is a trip," I said.

"Don't hold it against me." He laughed. "Mike can be a character, all right."

"Is he married?"

Aleck stopped dead in his tracks and let go of my hand. "What makes you ask that?"

"Women's intuition. It does exist, you know."

Aleck did not respond.

"It's cool," I said. "Nancy and Calibri really don't care; especially Nancy. They're only here to hang out and have fun. We're all grown."

He stared at me. "Aren't you going to ask me?"

"Ask you what?"

"If I'm married."

I shrugged. "Like I said, we're all grown."

I could tell that he was dying to ask me if I was married. There it was, on the tip of his tongue, but he swallowed it.

"Why'd you let go of my hand?" I asked. "I was enjoying that."

He took my hand back into his. "So, Los Angeles. Is it really as hot there as everyone claims?"

"You've never been to L.A.?"

"No, not yet. I've always planned to visit but haven't made it there yet." He smiled at me. "Maybe I'll have a reason to come now."

I cleared my throat uncomfortably. "Los Angeles has tricky weather. During the day, it can be hotter than hell and by nighttime, you might need a parka. It's beautiful, though."

"And obviously full of beautiful women to boot."

"Ooooh, Aleck, you have mad game."

We both laughed. "No, not me," he replied. "I simply recognize beauty when I see it; both inside and out."

In my entire life, I had been many things. Bold was never one of them. Yet, something overcame me at that very moment and it changed me.

"Aleck..."

"Yes?"

"There's something very sincere about you; something I want to experience...if only for one night."

"What do you mean, Kiss?"

We stopped in place while he awaited my answer. I took a deep breath, contemplating my next move.

"Do you believe in destiny?" I asked. "Like, do you believe that it's possible for two strangers to mesh so well together that it seems surreal? So much so that it seems like we've been in this place before?"

"I feel that way right now. I've felt it all day," he replied.

I wanted to feel him inside of me. Something about him made me feel so comfortable, so unique. I decided not to waste another moment of valuable time.

"Aleck?"

"Yes?"

"Would you like to fornicate under the consent of the king?"

ALECK

At first I thought that I was hearing things. Then she said it again. "Well, Aleck, would you like to fornicate under the consent of the king?"

The smile that spread across my face could have probably lit up the sky. "Kiss, it would be my pleasure but—"

"My pleasure, too." She placed her hand over my lips. "There are no buts...not tonight."